LKB
mcK.

THE MATING SEASON

The

MATING SEASON

ALEX BRUNKHORST

St. Martin's Press ☙ New York

www.stmartins.com

Library of Congress Cataloging-in-Publication Data

Brunkhorst, Alex
      The mating season / Alex Brunkhorst.—1st ed.
         p. cm.
      ISBN 0-312-31853-7
      EAN 978-0312-31853-6
      1. Women zoologists—Fiction. 2. Social isolation—Fiction. 3. Pet owners—
Fiction. 4. Architects—Fiction. I. Title.

PS3602.R85M38 2004
813'.6 22   2003069719

First Edition: July 2004

10 9 8 7 6 5 4 3 2 1

For Brad

ACKNOWLEDGMENTS

Thank you, first, to Leslie Falk at Collins McCormick Agency for being my agent and friend. Thank you also to Becki Heller, my editor, who always offered brilliant ideas and kind words. I am grateful to others at St. Martin's Press for their generous support and faith in the fairy tale world I have created, particularly Alicia Brooks, who believed from the beginning; Sally Richardson, publisher; John Cunningham, associate publisher; George Witte, editor in chief; Dori Weintraub, associate director of publicity; Christina Harcar, director of subsidiary rights; and Kevin Sweeney, production editor.

My real world is full of so many people who make it magical. I am grateful to all the early readers of the book and my extraordinary friends, particularly Robert Arakelian, Margaret Frohn, Evelyn Johnson, Rich Mutell, Blair Rich, and Christina Sun.

Lastly, among the brightest stars in my universe: Brad, you are a ray of light to me in a very dark world. And to my family—Mom, Dad, Vanessa, Austin, and Malcolm—thank you for always loving me despite my occasional complaining.

THE MATING SEASON

It was mating season, and Grasshopper was getting frisky. At first I thought his abrupt change in behavior was the result of Daylight Savings Time, a twice-yearly ritual that temporarily wreacked havoc on the entire menagerie. Each year, the sliding scale of the sun caused Butterfly to crash against the ceiling, as if suddenly forgetting the sky was no longer the limit. Tadpole nearly drowned; I had to gently, then more forcibly, prod him onto his green, heart-shaped life raft. Even Ant, my most resilient species, stumbled through October in desperate search for meaning. He usually found it in mid-November, in time for the leftover turkey and mashed potatoes I fed him after Thanksgiving.

But it was now the hour before the Festival. It was universally agreed that the Committee of Illumination—Hummingbird, Mockingbird, Bat, and Owl—had outdone itself this year. Chandeliers had been dimmed in favor of white teardrop lights, seaweed candles floated in the saltwater pond, and my stars had congregated just shy of the glass ceiling. It was said that Chairwoman Firefly, who had always been a micromanager of sorts, paid particular heed this year, and the house glistened with her touch.

Even more magnificent than the décor were my beloved creatures. They were in deep and serious preparation, standing before vanities and performing last-minute adjustments before venturing into the dark night to the Meadows *of Lophelia. Rabbit and Catfish fought over blue eyeliner, Mosquito practiced his strut, Daddy Long Legs assisted Tarantula in combing his radiant black coat. Ladybug, traditionally one of my more insecure creatures, had chosen a pink floor-length gown that showed off her single black spot. Bumblebee—Ladybug's best friend and a fashion devotee—advised against the choice, arguing that pink clashed with deep red; but Ladybug had been steadfast, and now Bumblebee felt a bit envious watching her dress in front of the three-way mirror. Dove asked for Moth's aid in hooking her top butterfly clasp; Jellyfish practiced his introduction (his date was known to be sea royalty); Peacock held a small bouquet of purple daisies that he would later present to his escort. There was a little bickering, some chiding, and a lot of teasing, but such antics were not surprising for a family of 310.*

There was music, too, a preamble to the twelve-piece orchestra that awaited at the Meadows of Lophelia. Some of the melody came from my creatures themselves: the aggressive chirp of Cricket, the chatter of Woodpecker, the slow hum of Veery Bird. Other harmonies gushed from my stars, a collective flicker of lights murmuring quietly.

Wings fluttered, antennae twitched, beady eyes looked at beady eyes. My creatures lined up single file, jockeying to be the first to the Meadows. The subtle notes of the cello, the throaty oboe, the whimsical flute; from acres away I could hear the symphonic beginnings of the Festival. My creatures heard it, too. Their laughter tickled the air. The Committee of Music, satisfied with the beginnings of Chopin's "Fantaisie in A Major," hovered near the front of the line. The Committee of Illumination, still intent on their duties, extinguished the candles and unplugged the white lights.

It took less than three minutes for the greenhouse to dim and go black, and another six for my creatures to line up. I looked at Millipede, the first creature in line, and opened the greenhouse door.

Although rumors and newspapers attest that daddies leave with a bang, most of the time they don't.

My eleventh birthday party began as a happy occasion, an intimate gathering of a few neighbor kids who hung around for the fried bologna sandwiches and party horns. Mama had prepared for the event: Varicolored confetti, goodie bags, and a fold-up "Happy Birthday" sign made our rundown living room seem as if it were waiting for something big. Mama had driven all the way into Ix to buy a piñata. She tied and untied and retied her apron all morning. My nerves were twitchy as well. I could not sit still.

Matty Munchau, a geeky kid with a premature bald spot on the crown of his head, arrived a few moments early. I was relieved he was the first; our discussions had always come relatively easily. We were discussing ionic structures when Lenny Lopate and Carrie Anselment arrived. Their moms had carpooled to the event, and I began to regret the whole party when I saw the snickering twosome walk up the concrete sidewalk. I blushed as I opened the door, and humbly accepted their presents wrapped in matching brown paper. Nikki Busby was next, then Joe Magnus. Mama bent down to kiss Daddy on the top of his head. "Our little girl's having a birthday party!" she said loudly, as if Daddy were someplace long distance or had lost his hearing. His ears worked perfectly, though, and he was right next to her in his armchair, focused on the baseball game on the television.

Lunch. Tag in the backyard. Pin the tail on the donkey. Goodie bags. Then, the piñata. Mama clapped her hands, as if to punctuate the exciting event, and we blindfolded Lenny with one of Daddy's old black socks and twirled him around three times.

"I feel dizzy," Lenny said, as he stumbled into the black-and-white television set, almost knocking it to the ground. Daddy's eyes grew wide and concerned, as if the baseball game were about to be called due to rain delay.

"Hey, hey, there," Daddy said to me, to Mama, to Lenny. I smiled a toothy grin at Daddy and quickly steered Lenny back to the center of the living room.

"Was that a ball or a strike?" Daddy said, as he turned up the volume of the television.

Mama giggled and retied her apron string in a big bow.

"Where is Joe?" she asked. We all (except for Lenny, of course) looked around. Joe Magnus was generally a loner, a kid who played solitary card games on the fifty-yard line of the football field at recess.

"I'll go find him," I said.

Joe was not hard to track down. He was in the kitchen, playing the primary school card game Go Fish, alone on the black-and-white tiled floor.

"Joe," I said tentatively, as speech was not something that came easily to me. "We're playing piñata. Lenny's . . ." I paused. What was Lenny exactly? "Blindfolded. I mean, *it.*"

Joe Magnus looked up from his card—Tuna, to be exact—and said, "Save a few caramels, please."

I nodded and left him alone. I had once been the girl version of that boy, but not now. It was my party.

We took turns at the piñata until Carrie finally batted it apart. The shower of candy fell in the pool of our giddy laughter. I was still afraid I'd say the wrong thing, as I often seemed to do, but as we tossed butterscotch chips, taffy, and grape balls into the air, my nerves almost disappeared.

When I returned to the kitchen with a handful of caramels, Joe's right hand was beating his left in Go Fish (Flounder was the clincher). I breathed in the air; it seemed festive, and I briefly wondered if air density varied by occasion. Happy Birthday air must be different from regular air: a bit more O_2, a pinch less CO_2, maybe even more Helium (He) because of all the balloons.

I was allergic to coconut, but it was Daddy's favorite cake and therefore the birthday party's centerpiece. Mama always took particular pride in this confection; she would carefully place candles on coconut cake even when no occasion called for such recognition, and she would feed Daddy the first bite. "This is how much I love you," Mama would say to Daddy, as she held up a cake full of tall lighted candles. For Mama, life with Daddy was a celebration deserving of capricious flames every day of the week.

But Mama had forgotten candles. She blamed the blunder on Todd Sunday—the bag boy at the market—but he was known to be very intent about his position, and I could not imagine he would have made such a mistake. The market was only a few minutes away, and Mama promised a speedy return.

One minute, four minutes, ten minutes slipped away. The kids—my new friends!—were restless now, and my nerves returned. The piñata was last hour's news; Julie had already eaten the homemade brownie from her goodie bag; Lenny called Matty a nerd and the insult's recipient had begun to cry. Candles suddenly seemed frilly and unnecessary. I only wanted Mama home again.

Daddy would be of no help, but desperation called me to seek him out. Although Mama had failed to notice, Daddy had been different in recent years. He was more interested in baseball now—he would eat Mama's famous meat loaf dinners in front of the television set, and grumble when she asked too many questions (particularly during extra innings). Although they had once been his hobby, Daddy neglected household chores. He no longer congratulated me on my report cards or attended school open houses. Mama's nagging came in the form of adoration, but it had driven Daddy to spend hours in Tap Whatever—his favorite local watering hole.

While the rest of the kids played in the front yard, I entered the living room. Daddy had an interest in sports; perhaps he could arrange an impromptu baseball game in the backyard or maybe even a loose game of kickball. Maybe he could discuss batting stats with the boys or give an abbreviated lecture on the perils of elk hunting. The seat of the armchair still held the indent of Daddy's blue jeans. Empty beer cans sat on the table in front of the chair, and *Decoys of the Papua Lakes*—Daddy's hunting hardbound—was open to a page on the North American duck. Three–zero, the television said. But the audience was gone.

I found Daddy sitting on the middle swing of our sturdy jungle gym. He had given this to me for my fourth birthday, and Mama often told me that Daddy had built it with his own two hands; he had not hired Hal's Hardware, like Jeannie Dunn's daddy had; he had not had Caroline's Toys deliver it in a single slab, as Clarence Michael's daddy had. No, said Mama, Daddy had kissed each screw, every nail, before he put them in.

"Daddy," I said as I stumbled into the outdoors. "Can you help? Mama went to the market because she forgot candles—well, she said Todd Sunday made the mistake, but he never makes bagging mistakes—and now . . ." I stopped to catch my breath. "Well, I was thinking you may help me by offering a lecture on elk hunting."

Daddy looked at me. His mouth resembled an upside-down U, his eyebrows right-side-up Vs. He carried a stuffed alligator.

"I bought you this," Daddy said, and handed me the animal. Despite his gruff mannerisms, the sheer size of him, he looked embarrassed. "But, I looked at your friends today, and I started to think maybe you're too old for stuffed animals. I got it at the toy store in town, so if you want . . ."

I hugged the stuffed alligator. He had green fur and triangular teeth clenched in concentration. Most of the people in my class didn't have stuffed animals anymore, but that was okay. I didn't have very many friends.

Daddy nodded, and traced the plaid in his workshirt. "You remind me of your grandma. You don't remember her."

I shook my head.

"She was really pretty—smart, too. Could have even gone to college if she hadn't met Pa."

"You could have gone to college, too, Daddy," I said, and the alligator looked up at me with wide-open eyes.

"Only thing I'm good for is baseball stats." He chuckled. Mama would have giggled at this, made him think that he had just delivered the best joke in the history of the world. I just nodded.

"I need to get going. Before Mom gets back with the candles."

"Where are you going? Aren't you going to stay for the rest of the party?" I asked. I had never been left alone before. Sometimes with a baby-sitter, but that didn't really count as alone.

"Mom will be home in a few minutes." Daddy paused here, as if to contemplate the word *minutes*. "Remember, Zorka, your life is your own. No one else's."

"I don't understand what . . ." I was going to begin, but Daddy wasn't listening. He wasn't really talking about me; he was talking about himself.

He headed past the side yard, the side with the blow-up kiddie pool and the tires from Mama's old Chevy. I heard the pickup sputter to life—the transmission was wearing out, he'd always say—then click into reverse. The AM radio faded out as the pickup left the driveway.

The truck was gone when Mama came home, but she was not worried. Assuming Daddy left for Tap Whatever, Mama cheerfully waited for his return. "Can we have birthday cake?" my new friends asked again and again. "As soon as Mr. Carpenter comes home. As soon as Mr. Carpenter comes home," she kept saying. Even after parents arrived and I politely excused myself to my bedroom, Mama sat in the kitchen alone beside the coconut cake with eleven unlit candles.

She waited the next morning, too. Her eyes hung heavy now, begging for sleep and a reprieve from worry. The cake with eleven candles kept her company; the coconut was already beginning to shrivel, the frosting to crystallize. Mama did not offer me a piece, and I returned home from school to find Mama still sitting by the coconut cake in darkness. The cake did not look like a cake anymore, but its candles still sat upright, waiting for fire.

"How was school, honey?" Mama asked, as if this were a usual day and her antics were normal.

"Fine. I received a gold star in science for my insights into the environmental benefits of the fern plant." I hugged the alligator closer to my chest.

"Good," she responded, and she fiddled with one of the candle's wicks. "I hope Daddy comes home soon. The cake is going to get stale."

I nodded in collusive agreement and excused myself to my bedroom. I looked at my alligator. Daddy wasn't coming home.

Once in my bedroom, I closed the creaky door, changed out of my school clothes, and opened my backpack as if it contained a sought-after treasure or something wicked.

The Encyclopedia of Animals was a scary-looking text, even for me. Everything about the blue thousand-plus pager intimidated: its Gothic-looking font, the red circular sticker that screamed "For Intermediate Readers Only," the nonglossied paper, the deliberately monotone pictures (apparently intermediate readers no longer liked or demanded color depictions). Despite all these warnings—or perhaps to spite them—I had checked the book out of the school library that morning.

An open crease led to giraffes, tigers, day geckoes, aardvarks, chipmunks, betta fish, bluebirds, ants. The smallest specimens and the largest. The meanest, the moodiest, the most docile. Animals I would not want to meet in a dark alley and some I already had. I suddenly felt as if I were in the hard jungles of Africa, on the mosquito-infested shores of the Nile. I moved the alligator so he could see better, too, and pointed to a picture of his cousin, the awe-inspiring crocodile.

My alligator's eyes grew wider.

"The crocodile," I began, watching his reaction, "is a close relative of the alligator. Certain of its more ferocious species have been known to attack man. . . ."

And a new world began to open up for me.

I

Zorka is my name. It is a family name, my paternal grandmother's to be exact, and was for many years my favorite
part of me. While my grandmother was embarrassed by her
name and adopted "Mary" in its stead, I always felt that Zorka was a
name that belonged in print—"In Typical Act of Heroism, Czarina
Zorka Incites One-Woman Coup and Frees Peasants." "Billionaire
Oil Tycoon Blackwell Dies, Heiress Zorka 'Inconsolable.'" "Zeus to
Marry Goddess Zorka in Civil Ceremony."

My grandmother was invented before the airbrush but photographs still portray her as beautiful. I wish I looked like her, had her
white bouffant hair and salmon-colored lips, but I do not. Because of
my lofty pedigree (Mama had been a local beauty queen and Daddy
looked like Robert Redford), my makings had all the right ingredi-
ents—blond hair, blue eyes, long limbs—but things must have gone
wrong in the cooling process, for the results were less than spectacular.
I was subservient to this fact. I never had time to dedicate emotional
resources to a petty thing like beauty.

I devoted each and every hour of my day to animals. While my
fellow class members went to dances, listened to rock and roll, kissed

for the first time, I sponged up words, diagrams, and pictures. When I was left alone on the playground, I would repeat animal facts in my mind: The domestic dog differs from the gray wolf by 0.2 percent of mtDNA sequence. Seahorses can be bred in captivity if they have access to a steady flow of mysis shrimp. The peacock mates in the rainy season. Ceilings in the faraway island of Madagascar are the day geckoes' playground.

Due to quite a few skipped grades, I was the youngest girl in my class at Ix Public. I was little for my grade, and I often found myself tongue-tied in even the most basic of nonscientific conversations. The occasional kid—coincidentally the same guy who played with Bunsen burners on weekends or knew the molecular structure of obscure elements like praseodymium—would engage me in conversation or organize a study group with me as its moderator. But generally, I was an outcast. I was picked last for Red Rover. The gym teacher, not a fellow student, held my ankles while I did sit-ups. Lunchtime, too, only brought loneliness: I sat at the end of the table alone with my alligator and ate a peanut butter and jelly sandwich while reading a science text.

Ix Public was a magnet school, attracting wealthy and privileged children from the big city, children who lived in tall skyscrapers and drove to school in the backs of cars with silver hood ornaments and drivers who weren't their parents. Then there were the kids like me—kids who were raised in Unity and had never even seen the big city, let alone played on its twenty-fourth floors and dined in its pricey restaurants. Sometimes I felt as if Ix Public was one big social awareness experiment.

Despite my young age, I was the grade's most advanced student. Due to extreme shyness, I rarely raised my hand; nevertheless, I quickly earned the title of class-know-it-all. Teachers would weed through the kids who eagerly professed to have a firm grasp of the answer and look

to me, hand glued to the desk, for the correct one. I often willed myself to offer up the wrong response in order to ingratiate myself to my
potential friends—"Zorka, what is H_2O?" "Sodium Nitrate," I would
reply in my daydreams. But in the end, it was similar to driving off a
bridge. Unless your brakes were faulty and your foot was tied to the
gas pedal, it was just too great a leap.

When the school bus came to a screeching halt, I was reading the animal encyclopedia. We were so accustomed to the "For Sale by Own-
er" sign outside the gated residence that we had overlooked the sign's
absence until now. The circa '50s estate had been most likely transported to Ix from Las Vegas—lions, crested gates, and all. It had stood
lonely for years, and kids tossed about rumors of ghosts, its sordid past,
and nebulous future (the doom-filled words "razed for a children's
center" were not unfamiliar).

Now, though, a diminutive girl with a side part, coke-bottle glasses,
and a thickly bound textbook stood in front of the residence at a new
bus stop. The girl looked of Northeastern Asian descent and wore all
khaki. Her parents stood directly behind her, their transfixed gazes
similar to those of Biblical pagans as they prayed to false, golden idols.

The mother and father bowed deeply before their daughter, an ancient gesture that served as her cue to ascend the school bus steps. The
red lights of the stop sign blinked brightly, casting a spotlight on the
self-important teen. A sea of astonished faces stared at her; she took
the liberty of sitting beside mine.

A ruler was tucked behind the girl's ear measuring centimeters,
not inches.

"Pardon?" she asked of me, tossing out a word meant to be used at
dinner parties by the bourgeoisie.

"Pardon," I responded, flipping her question into the affirmative.

The answer did not matter, for she was already seated. "I . . ."—she paused here—"am Kris Tina Woo." Kris Tina Woo did not present her hand; instead, she offered a quick nod of the head, a flippant bow.

"Hello, Christina," I responded. It was the first time I had been approached on the school bus, and I did not want to alienate, well, this alien girl.

"No." She shook her head, dislodging the ruler from its nest between her shiny hair and little ear. "Not right at all. Repeat after me: Kris Tina Woo."

"Christina Woo," was my perplexed response.

"No. First name: Kris. Second name: Tina. Last name: Woo."

"Oh," I said.

"I come to Ix Public by way of Seoul, Korea." Kris Tina paused, and she pulled out a text with weird symbols from her bag. It featured a picture of a glassy building on the cover.

I focused on a daddy long legs who had accompanied her onto the bus. He appeared to be enjoying the bus ride. I picked him up and pet his little belly. He giggled, but Kris Tina didn't hear; he flailed his legs in the air, but no one noticed.

"Do you have a name?" Kris Tina asked with blatant, ninth-grade sarcasm.

"Zorka," I answered, blushing.

"That's a strange name. Is it American?"

This was a question I had never considered. "Yes," I replied. "I think so."

"I see. Mother, Father, and I happened to note your stares." She was referring to the collective "your" here, not just mine. "Were you looking at The Woo Residence?"

"I think we were . . ." I faded out here, not knowing how to respond. "Well, I think we were looking at the house with the cement lions. It was for sale before."

"That is The Woo Residence. All Modernist homes have names."

"Modernist?"

Kris Tina Woo, of The Woo Residence, nodded her head. It was a condescending, almost pandering gesture, indicating she was about to state the obvious.

"Yes, The Woo Residence is Modernist. It even has a flat roof."

Kris Tina must have realized I was an uninformed audience for she turned back to her well-worn textbook. Page 176 featured a picture of a skyscraper. It was cut off at the middle—at floor twenty-one perhaps. Kris Tina referred to her ruler and began to scribble down measurements.

Kris Tina didn't look up, instead continuing her explanation, "I am to assume you have no idea what Modernism is."

I shrugged.

"Well, architectural Modernism was a movement." She stressed this word. "The basis of it is the unification of nature and where we live and work."

I guess I still looked confused—because I was—as Kris Tina continued, "Modernist architects achieve this goal by using large windows to soften the transition between indoor and outdoor light, unframed windows that become invisible in the wall plane. They use affordable materials as well"—she looked at me with disgust—"so even the commoner can afford their vision."

I had no idea what she was talking about; therefore, I craned my neck toward the picture in her architecture book and squinted to see its details.

"This is in Beijing, a place I am certain you have never been." Kris Tina did not look up from the diagram, instead referring to the ruler's millimeter line with a magnifying glass she had retrieved from her backpack. "Beijing is in China and this is its most famous monument."

"Isn't that where the Great Wall is?" I asked. Kris Tina allowed me a closer look at her text. The skyscraper was glass and, oddly, incomplete.

Kris Tina stared at the skyscraper as her parents had stared at her just four bus stops earlier—with astonished admiration. "I want to be one someday."

I looked at the page filled with Kris Tina's margin comments, which consisted of perfectly written notes to self and exclamation points (*Note to self: Use glass!*).

"You want to be a skyscraper?" I asked naïvely.

The daddy long legs was getting jittery and threatened to escape via the bus window. I coddled him in my palm.

"No, silly." Kris Tina looked at me with disgust, and then smiled like a girl whose ego weighed more than her frame. "I want to be an architect."

II

The future was not what it used to be.

Soon after Daddy left, Mama had begun going to St. Bernard's 7:45 A.M. mass. At first I was satisfied with this progress, as I felt Mama was more productive in church than sitting at our kitchen table. Perhaps she could meet other women who also sat beside stale cakes awaiting the return of their husbands.

But as months went by, it became clear that church was not a place one went to become normal again. Like her heart, Mama's mind seemed to be cracking. Toting a rosary, she prayed to obscure saints (St. Helen, for example). She erroneously assumed lesser-known saints received fewer requests than God Himself, thus had more time to answer them. She stopped sleeping in favor of pacing the overgrown and weedy rose garden; her signature lilac eye shadow ran purple with tears. The market was too ambitious a task; Todd Sunday—a fellow member of St. Bernard's—delivered groceries directly to the house. Mama often talked to him about Daddy, recounting the same story of the day they had met. Sometimes she even put on the powder blue dress she wore that day to make the account more real.

Mama believed that if we wanted Daddy to come home, it was essential that Jesus be aware that I wanted this as well; she thought two people's prayers were better than one. Therefore, every day Mama pulled me from first period at school, dressing me in my Sunday best, and together we went to the sparsely attended morning mass. She rambled about Daddy and Jesus and prayers, bowing her head in deep reverie, pulling her skirt up slightly to feel the hard, sacrificial wood of the kneeler. When she sensed my ambivalence to the ritual, she glared at me with the eyes of a jack-o'-lantern.

It was a stormy day. Surprised by the tentative but rapid knock on the door, I gingerly called out, "Who's there?" The response, "God's representatives," was both odd and unnerving. I was not ready for God's representatives quite yet; I was in the middle of researching the idiosyncrasies of the vinegar fly. I had imported eight examples of the species from the local woods, and they rested on our living room floor, nibbling carpet wool. I glanced out the peephole. A big silver cross with a very vivid picture of Jesus stared back at me.

Mama was not at home, I told Sister Jean and Pastor Bob as I answered the flimsy door. Mama had long ceased doing even the simplest of tasks; since the screen door was off its hinges, I lifted it, placing it on the cement steps. There was nothing between Mama, me, and the rest of the world anymore.

Despite Mama's absence, Sister Jean and Pastor Bob entered. Along with the eight vinegar flies, a centipede, a ladybug, and a sagebrush vole crawled on the floor. God's representatives exchanged glances as I politely invited them to sit on the creature-free sofa. I thought I saw Sister Jean make a quick sign of the cross. The sole beverage in the house was water from the faucet, which I poured into two tall glasses with perfectly drawn polka dots. Ice fancied the water a bit, made it somehow seem less tap. The creatures' bulb eyes were trained on the television set, except for the ladybug, who was napping.

Sister Jean and Pastor Bob knew that Mama was not at home—she was at a prayer group on the Acts of the Apostles—and they also sensed she was very sick. They added this part as an afterthought, as if Mama being very sick was less important than her learning about the Acts of the Apostles. I glanced at the creatures. The ladybug was breathing heavily in sleep; the vinegar flies' red eyes matched her shell.

The real reason for this visit, continued the Sister and the Pastor, was to discuss with me Mama's rest of kin. Mama needed to be in a hospital, maybe even one in another county. Her condition was precarious. She had an illness of the mind, they explained, but Mama did not recognize it herself. It was kind of like looking at yourself in the mirror; you can't see your own back. I crinkled my forehead at the poor analogy.

I smiled and addressed God's representatives with false aplomb. No, I was not aware of any family who could assist us. I was sensitive to the issue, I asserted, and I would gladly keep my ears open for stray relatives who might be willing to commit Mama. In my heart, though, I was angry. I was not grown-up yet, and all this responsibility seemed too much to bear. Mama would never go to a hospital, and Sister Jean and Pastor Bob should have known that. She would not go because she still believed Daddy was coming back.

Sister Jean and Pastor Bob then asked about me—an addendum to Mama's illness, which had been an afterthought to the Acts of the Apostles. I was well, I lied, busily tending to my life, my studies, and my friends. "I sometimes feel as if there is so much tugging at me," I said, "so many aspects of adolescence demanding my time and attention." I silently apologized to Sister Jean's cross when I said this, as I knew lying (even fibs of the white variety) to Holy People was a greater sin than lying to laity.

I did not escort the Sister and the Pastor to the door. It was open, after all, though it only led to a closed world. Instead, I lazily joined the creatures on the carpeted floor, stretching out as far as my extremities would allow. I was finally growing, and I sensed I would eventually be very tall. Perhaps someday I would be the length of the entire living room.

I allowed the creatures outside to play. They sprinted, galloped, flew away from the house, whatever their individual mode of transport. I watched them until they disappeared.

III

Typically, Mr. Aloni—our Sociology teacher—was a hard-nosed individual who shunned what he termed "soft homework." Mr. Aloni's definition of soft homework was all-encompassing: anything involving pie charts, interviewing local celebrities, clippings from newspapers, et cetera. He looked with disdain at students completing such assignments (sometimes going as far as tapping their wrists with rulers), and expressed contempt for teachers who were the perpetrators of such "time-wasting endeavors" (an actual quote from a faculty meeting).

It was thus that Mr. Aloni's annual field-trip assignment was particularly odd. The Ix Public student body always looked forward to the assignment; it not only meant a day out of classes, but also an opportunity to socialize with friends during school hours.

The project was straightforward. We were to take another person to some place of significance in our lives.

In the past, students had been to grandparents' gravesites, to the Ix Gardens, to quiet places like churches or to noisy ones like the big city or to trash-infested ones like the Unity Pond. Kris Tina Woo had eagerly chosen me as her partner and, as I had strongly suspected, her

choice of locale directly related to the blue textbook which ubiqui-
tously adorned her right arm.

Mr. Woo picked me up at exactly 8:00 A.M. I slithered into the
backseat next to Kris Tina. She sat with her textbook on her lap and
seemed very excited.

"Hello, Zorka. It only occurred to me after we spoke last evening
that perhaps I should have presented you with this"—she lifted her blue
text—"in order that you could be well prepared for today's excursion."

I could not imagine anything I would have liked less than to read
Kris Tina's architecture textbook, but I nodded.

"Perhaps I could purchase one?" I asked.

"I wish that were the case, but it's out of print," Kris Tina said.

"That's a shame."

"It is. A dirty shame."

"Do you mind if I look at the book for a moment?"

Kris Tina gingerly handed me the book.

The skyscraper on the cover—the half that still stood, at least—was
impressive, so glassy the sun appeared to shine right through it. The
book's title, *Dorsey: The Unfinished Works,* was written in bold print. I
gave the book back to Kris Tina. She was finally able to exhale again.

"I know I may seem a bit, well, possessive, of this text." Kris Tina
looked out the window, and seemed suddenly sad. "But, see, as I mentioned, it is out of print and . . ."

The landscape passed by the moving car. It was almost as if we
were not moving forward, but the landscape was moving backward. "I
wonder if a long time ago, he could have been like me."

Suddenly life seemed to be going by very quickly.

Kris Tina continued, "You see, Architect Dorsey was someone
with his life ahead of him, but then something happened and everything fell apart."

I nodded and suddenly I, too, was overwhelmed with sadness. We were really far away from civilization; we passed cows, purple wildflowers, train tracks, silos. The countryside was full of things built a long time ago, things which seemed to serve little purpose today.

I must have fallen asleep in the car, for three hours later, I awoke to Kris Tina's little hands shaking my shoulders.

"We're here!"

In the remote landscape stood the most beautiful building I had ever seen. Even as an architecture novice, I could appreciate that this was the work of someone with incredible talent. To quote Kris Tina Woo, someone of genius. The glass structure was probably forty stories tall, hourglass-shaped, and its top was jagged. It stopped mid-floor, as if a very large saw or scissors were used to cut off the top of the building and take it far away, shattering Architect Dorsey's dreams.

The lonely structure was surrounded by weeds, prickly wild plants stories in height.

"This is Dorsey Monument One." Kris Tina pulled her ruler from behind her ear and held it perpendicular to the horizon. She grabbed binoculars from her canvas bag. Although she had obviously been to Dorsey Monument One before, it was as if the girl were looking at it for the first time.

"It's breathtaking," I said.

Kris Tina nodded, as if the skyscraper were of her own design. "Thank you."

I allowed her to spend a moment in silence with the Monument. A tear settled in Kris Tina's eye, and she pulled a linen khaki handkerchief from her bag.

"Architect Dorsey started no fewer than nine monuments before . . . well, before he ceased being an architect. This was the first." Kris Tina paused, regaining her composure. She took my hand in hers, and moved me closer to the magnificent structure. The weeds around it were dense and thick; Kris Tina had conveniently brought a pair of weed clippers.

"Why are there so many weeds?" I asked. "Doesn't anyone take care of it?"

Kris Tina began snipping. "Coincidentally, you reference one of the great enigmas of this specific Dorsey design." I felt her fingers squeeze mine as we continued into the now clipped clearing.

Inside the clearing, I could better see the Monument; its lower floors and the yellow *Danger* tape which separated it from mankind.

"Note the soil," Kris Tina began, as she leaned down and ran the dirt through her fingers. I followed her lead. The soil was not soil at all; it was mud. "As you are aware, we are in the desert. As a matter of fact, it hasn't rained here in months." Kris Tina paused for a moment, like a magician before pulling a white rabbit from his hat. "But the ground around this specific monument is always wet and the weeds around it grow at a ferocious pace. Museums have attempted to take control of the property and curtail the growth, but it is impossible."

"But," I began, "how can that be? Can't they monitor for rain?"

"They've tried. But it's almost as if . . ." Kris Tina bit the end of her ruler. "The rain knows when they're monitoring and stops. I know it sounds silly, but . . . well . . . let's talk about the architectural significance of the Monument."

Two hours passed and the weeds didn't grow, but Kris Tina Woo, with the assistance of her textbook, painstakingly explained the significance of Dorsey Monument One. The Monument was commissioned by a soft drink mogul who had astonished the world by choosing the nineteen-year-old architect to design the vast structure. The man had made his bold decision off a simple, two-foot jar the young Dorsey had designed in bronze for an intermediate vessel class.

Dorsey Monument One replicated the glass bottle which housed the soft drink, and it did so in exact scale. The structure was lauded not only for its revolutionary design, but also for Dorsey's expert handling of natural light (moonlight, starlight, sunlight all looked the same from inside, so worker productivity skyrocketed).

"Off this design, Architect Dorsey received commissions to design eight additional monuments. Skyscrapers in Beijing, Iceland, Oslo, Belize, Cape Town, Riyadh. A war memorial in Iran. And a single residence in an undisclosed location. None of these were completed, however." Kris Tina paused, looked up. "He always designed in glass, yet only in this monument is it clear he hadn't yet quite made peace with the material." Kris Tina pointed to a single prism, on the tenth floor. To my untrained eye, it looked beautiful, but it must have been a mistake. She continued, "He was young, though."

"What happened?" I asked. I did not mean the glass glitch. Kris Tina understood.

"So much fanfare." She said this nostalgically, as if she had witnessed it. "They even thought he would win the Pritzker, but then, then, he just stopped. He blamed a flaw in the design, but no one has ever been able to find it, not even in the blueprints. He began his next monument in Beijing but . . ." Kris Tina opened her blue textbook to the page on Beijing. She pointed, with her ruler, to the half-completed Chinese skyscraper. "Architect Dorsey was never able to complete a single monument. He eventually dropped out of architecture school. The world was stunned."

I was overwhelmed with an emotion I could not put into words. It was as if I suddenly felt a connection to a man I had never met.

Kris Tina Woo looked at the top of the Monument. Its zigzagged end.

"At nineteen he designed this." Kris Tina made a sweeping gesture toward the skyscraper in front of us and to Beijing, Iceland, Oslo, Belize, Cape Town, Riyadh, Iran, and the undisclosed location of the single residence. "And then . . ." She faded out, like he had.

I understood that Mr. Aloni's Sociology assignment wasn't soft homework at all. Surely, on the surface the assignment wasn't as intellectually stimulating as frog dissection in Biology or Shakespeare readings in AP English. Yet, in some weird way, Mr. Aloni's homework assignment was the hardest of them all, and its lesson the most salient. For, in the end, despite our differences, we were all the same; we were all scared of becoming *that person*. Kris Tina Woo was afraid of becoming Architect Dorsey, a man who had somehow lost everything, mid-skyscraper.

"People have conjectured as to why, of course. Some said it was a family tragedy, others said he was afraid of his own potential, some speculated it was something as mundane as procrastination. But no one was ever certain."

"What do you think?" I asked.

"I don't know," she replied. "But eventually, eventually I want to find out for sure."

A storm was on the horizon, and I wondered if one day a natural force would tear apart the structure. Only nine examples of Architect Dorsey's quashed dreams remained, and I suddenly wished they were small enough to be transported to museums.

On the way back to Unity, I skimmed through *Dorsey: The Unfinished Works*, but discovered very little else about the enigmatic architect. The text was architecture focused, offering little in the way of biographical information, and ended at the noncompletion of Architect Dorsey's final known work: Dorsey Monument Eight. It was in Belize, and the architect's visits to the faraway country coincided with the North American winter, as he preferred warm, sunny weather. The text referenced the one residence he designed, but did not feature a pictorial on the home. Instead, the author painstakingly explained that the residence was designed for an unknown client and was, at present, yet to be located. Questions centered on whether the home even existed. Architect Dorsey, who refused to be interviewed, would never discuss his designs or personal life with the public.

IV

Even in the earliest years of grammar school, a quiet wind followed Zoë Christie. Her hair was always gelled back with the latest in expensive mousse, lest it flow into her violet eyes and hinder her ability to discern the "right people" from the "wrong." The light breeze that ran through Zoë's hair must have been a head wind, for it caused her to stroll with a slow deliberation, as if her destination were in some way a necessary evil. Zoë's nose always pointed sixty-two degrees into the air. In addition to its obvious effects on Zoë's glorious blond hair and gait, the wind whirling about Zoë must have affected her metabolic rate as well, for despite professing her love for expensive French cheeses and caviar, food only influenced Zoë's height, not her weight.

Fate—more specifically, perfect alignment—was the force that pulled Zoë and me together. Our teacher, Miss Kastle, was a fanatic of order; chairs were centered on the floor as if the tiles were rulers, chalk arranged according to the colors of the rainbow, birthdays marked clearly on otherwise unmarked calendars. Miss Kastle believed in order for her students as well—alphabetical order by first name, to be exact.

Thus, my life became inexorably intertwined with that of Zoë Christie, the only other Z in the tenth grade.

Zoë's every movement reeked of popularity. Even if she had wanted to (which she obviously did not), she could not have denied her pedigree, for it was the kind that was built over generations.

"Hey," Zoë whispered. We were in the hall line and she nudged me aggressively. It was not intrusive. No one had ever nudged me before.

"Yes?" I answered. The response tickled with nerves.

"Zorka's kind of a cool name. Where did you get it?"

"My parents," I answered dumbly. I immediately regretted my response and wanted to swallow it.

"No, I mean, is it an actress's name or something? My daddy took me to New York last year, and I think I may have seen it outside of a play."

I contemplated this. I had two choices. Lie and earn Zoë's respect, or tell the truth and lose it.

"It was my grandmother's name," I said honestly. "She was very beautiful, though, and could have been on stage if she had wanted to. She decided to be a wife instead."

"Oh," Zoë said as she flipped a wisp of blond hair out of her eye. "I wish I had been named for someone else. I think it gives you someone to live up to. My parents had wanted to name one of their horses Zoë but it didn't work out, so I got it."

"It's a very beautiful name," I said. My tone was calmer now, and it exuded something just short of confidence. "Your name is a literary name. It reminds me of Zooey in *Franny and Zooey*."

"What is that?" Zoë asked as the shrill of the hall bell interrupted our discussion.

Our clandestine conversations continued in line after line, class-room after classroom. Although Zoë and I became instant friends, she insisted our friendship remain closeted. I did not blame her for being furtive, as I could not imagine being in the position to even have to make such a judgment call. My friendship with Zoë soon transcended the school halls, and I was invited to socialize at her country estate. The Christie's driver came to pick us up at school in a long black car, and he was allowed to the front of the line, even before the buses. He opened the back door, and Zoë slithered into the black leather seats. I followed her lead, and the car door was closed behind me by a hand I didn't see.

"My daddy is a businessman," Zoë began as she applied a fresh coat of lipstick in preparation for her demanding mother. "He commutes all the way to the big city so that I may spend more time with Winnie."

"Winnie?" I asked. "I thought you were an only child."

"Winnie is my horse," Zoë said. "I ride her almost every day."

"You have a horse?" I asked incredulously. Zoë was beautiful and popular and wore fancy clothes, but the thought that she had a horse who she could talk to and spend time with made me jealous. I wouldn't have even needed friends if I had a horse.

"Yes, I have her because I live on an equestrian estate," Zoë said to the rearview mirror before informing the driver, through a series of complex eye movements, to slow down so she could accurately draw her jet black eyeliner. "But it isn't an estate in the typical sense of the word—it is an architectural estate, like falling water."

I nodded in agreement, although I did not know with what I was agreeing.

"Will I be able to meet Winnie?" I asked eagerly.

"If her schedule allows. She's a very busy horse, you know," Zoë said. She smiled into the rearview mirror and the newly beautified Zoë Christie smiled back. "The stable hands take her to shows. Mommy and Daddy get angry if she loses; they say it looks bad in front of their friends."

"Is she at a show today?" I asked.

"We'll ask the stable hands when we arrive," Zoë said.

Zoë's equestrian estate was beautiful, but I didn't understand how it looked like falling water. The house was built into the hill, and the construction workers must have forgotten to take out the boulders in the living room because they were still there. When we arrived, Zoë's mommy was in the living room, talking to a sleek black leather chair.

"Now, you would look great over next to the sofa. Don't you think?" she asked the chair. Zoë seemed used to this.

The chair didn't answer, but Zoë did. "Mommy, you've had the chair next to the sofa before. Remember, you didn't like it?" Zoë gave her mommy a little kiss on the back of her diamonded neck; it was the kiss of a teenager who wasn't supposed to like her mommy but did anyway.

Mrs. Christie tore her eyes from the furniture and looked at Zoë and then me. She wetted her fingers with her tongue and patted down a stray hair which had intruded upon Zoë's face.

"Zoë, heart, who is this?" Mrs. Christie asked condescendingly. An end table would have received more respect, by a lot.

"Her name is Zorka. She's really smart and is helping me with my homework," Zoë responded promptly. The question had been anticipated, the answer rehearsed. "Where is Winnie?" Zoë continued.

Soon after, we were escorted to the stables and I was introduced to Winnie. She was standing in her stall when we arrived. She whinnied loudly and shook her head; Zoë appeared disgusted by it all.

"Winnie is a green horse, which means she isn't well behaved yet," Zoë said, motioning to the saddle hand to open the stall. Zoë stepped back in anticipation.

The saddle hand approached the door, and Winnie slammed her hoof into the side of the stable. Hay flew. I looked at Winnie, and she quieted a bit. Her eyes turned docile.

"Can I let her out?" I asked the stable hand. "I think horses like me."

Before he could answer, I approached Winnie and offered her the back of my hand. After a moment of hesitation, she licked it. My hand was now sloppy and wet, which made me giggle.

"That tickles," I said to Winnie. In response, she again licked my hand and moved closer to me. I unlatched the side of the door and Zoë walked backward nervously. Winnie, though, stood still and looked out to the riding ring.

The stable hand and Zoë watched in awe. Winnie proudly stood erect, her chest pushed to the sky and her legs still. I led her away from the barn. "I want to show you something," I said.

The violet field was dense and wild and exactly matched the color of Zoë Christie's eyes. I had noticed the patch of purple when we had driven into the estate, but it looked even more magnificent up close. Each individual flower was a combination of purple, yellow, and green. It humbled anything man-made, including Zoë Christie's vast architectural estate.

I held a single violet up to Winnie's nose so she could experience what it was like to live someplace faraway. She smelled the flower and the hair on her mane stood straight on edge. She whinnied gently.

"I have a secret to tell you," I said to her and she leaned closer to me, so close that I could feel the fur of her ear on my lips.

Zoë ended up at my house for dinner quite by accident. Zoë's daddy was a hunter, and I had mentioned to Zoë that her daddy may enjoy *Decoys of the Papua Lakes,* a duck hunting book my Daddy had committed to memory when he was still around. Zoë had accepted the gift and volunteered to stop by to pick it up.

Mama was feisty that evening, rambling about Grandmother Zorka and complaining about the tomato soup I had prepared. But when Zoë rang the doorbell, Mama invited her to join us for our meal and Zoë surprisingly accepted.

"So, Mrs. Carpenter, are you involved with any local charities?" Zoë asked. Her question cut the silence like a knife.

"No, I'm not. I guess I'm what you'd call a charity case myself," Mama answered enigmatically. I stared at her as a mother might look at a child who misbehaves in church. Oblivious to my reprimand, Mama continued. "That's really nice of you to come over. Zorka doesn't have any friends, poor thing."

I felt my face burn hot, like coals over a fire. Zoë, as trained by her mother, remained polite and stoic.

"She was so nice in volunteering to let me bring *Decoys of the Papua Lakes* to Daddy. He loves duck hunting and will find this most interesting."

Mama glared at me. "That's your daddy's favorite book. He'll be furious if it isn't here when he gets home," she said.

Zoë swallowed her bite of soup and put the water glass to her lips, as if giving herself a reason to remain silent.

"Mama, Daddy isn't coming home," I said. "This book has been lying on the end table for years."

This infuriated her. "He most certainly is coming home. In fact, he'll be here any minute now," Mama responded.

"You're not making any sense. Daddy's gone," I said.

"You're the one not making any sense." Mama directed this comment at me, and then refocused on Zoë. "Honey, I'm really sorry about Zorka's behavior. She doesn't seem to realize what she's saying."

"That's okay," Zoë said. "I didn't really need the book anyway. Daddy can always buy one. He has a fairly extensive hunting library."

"No, you should take the book." My reaction was very different from Zoë's when her mother was speaking to furniture. Mine acknowledged the blatant insanity. Perhaps Zoë did not believe this, though.

Zoë looked at her gold watch. "I should really be going. Mommy and Daddy will be upset if I don't get home to brush Winnie. There's a lot of responsibility in having a horse. Sometimes I forget that I have more than myself to think about."

Thirty seconds later, Zoë left. I tried calling her estate, but her governess said she was visiting Winnie in her stable. The next morning, I arrived to school early and waited at our side-by-side lockers.

I did not understand it at first. Certainly, I could interpret the symbolism in the twenty-eight stuffed, wooden, and plastic ducks that sat on my desk, but I could not understand cruelty. I sat down silently while my twenty-eight classmates watched; the kindest sat in silence, the meanest sneered and chortled. I finally garnered the nerve to look at Zoë.

She was doing her Earth Science homework and fiddling with her gold ring. It had belonged to her grandmother, I remembered her telling me, and she had always said it made her smarter and a bit more lovely.

V

Zoë flipped through her textbooks and glanced at herself in the antique mirror her family's interior designer had hung in her locker. A stray hair had flown in Zoë's eyes; she sprayed a bit of hairspray on it and attempted to fasten it back in a diamond barrette. All endeavors failed, however, and exasperation set in. Zoë looked to me as if I was the ready solution to the problem, but one she could not use without risking embarrassment.

"I hate early eighteenth-century mirrors." Zoë's displeasure prodded her voice up a few levels. It was still hushed, however; one would have to strain to hear her anger. "Mommy is hiring a new interior designer, and the first thing he is going to do is replace this. Even before he finds new pool chaises."

I looked up, questioningly.

"This piece of glass distorts me. I guess French women didn't need to see themselves." Zoë continued, "I am more than certain, however, that Mr. Dorsey will find the perfect midcentury piece."

For the first time in my high school existence, I heard Zoë speak reverently of another soul. Her inflection was melodic, as if she heard song in his name.

"Did I hear you say Architect Dorsey?" Kris Tina Woo's question came from twenty lockers away and reeked of eagerness, excitement, and terror.

"I am truly vexed," Zoë said, ignoring the question and again struggling with her barrette. "I may just have to go home, to the architectural estate, sick."

And with that, Zoë slammed her antique-filled locker and headed to the nurse's office.

Four days later, Zoë's antique mirror was replaced. Zoë looked particularly glorious; it was almost as if she had dressed up to look more beautiful in front of her new, streamlined piece of glass. Zoë stared at the mirror as if it had suddenly turned to twenty-four carat gold.

"Mr. Dorsey did a genius job on the locker installation. Wouldn't you agree?" Her speech was nuanced, like when the French spoke "n'est-ce pas."

I looked at the locker. Each of Zoë's textbooks had been covered in brown paper with tiny black type denoting its subject matter (Algebra was simply "Mathematics"; Biology, "Science"; French, "Français."). The superfluous decorations and chintz locker paper—apparently the choices of her previous designer—were gone. The locker once again looked brown, like ours.

The locker's sole decoration was a single orchid. It sat atop the texts and it was white.

Zoë continued, "He even bought me this orchid. He claimed it was part of the installation, but I am certain he bought it for me because orchids are rather erotic."

The silk lime green knee-length dress; the shimmering choice of eye shadow; the excessive accessorizing with diamonds: this was beginning to make sense.

"You mean exotic?" I asked.

"You always have to look for the negative, Zorka," Zoë said, as she fingered the orchid. "Mr. Dorsey's going to be spending more time at the architectural estate now. Mommy told him to do the installation gradually. Although this is usually not his preferred method of work he acquiesced." Zoë smiled and the twinkle in her eye bounced off the sleek mirror.

"I see."

"Mr. Dorsey said the locker brown is a very nice pantone."

"I can see his point." I nodded, although I didn't see his point at all.

"So why cover something so brilliant with chintz?" Zoë asked this question rhetorically—she was probably quoting Mr. Dorsey directly—and I looked at my own locker. Unbeknownst to Zoë, a centipede and a mosquito had accompanied me to school. They now played in my brown pantone locker with some leaves I had brought in. I smiled at the little insects and they smiled back.

"Zorka," Zoë began, and I could not imagine a girl ever looking more beautiful. She could have even been a fashion model. "Now that Mr. Dorsey will be spending more time at the architectural estate with me, we will have to limit your visits."

Even though Mrs. Christie talked to furniture and Zoë was self-absorbed, I loved spending time at Zoë's house. Winnie was there, of course, and the horse had recently taken me to a lake on the premises where a million fish swam.

"You may come over the night before tests, so we can study together." Zoë paused and applied more lilac eye shadow. "You may also come over on weekends when Mr. Dorsey is out of town. He is doing a house in Santa Fe at the moment so his travel schedule is quite heavy."

Zoë gazed once again at her locker before closing it with the tenderness a mother reserves for handling her newborn.

———

"Faster, Zorka."

Mr. Dorsey was in Santa Fe on business, and I had been invited to the architectural estate. Zoë had been a bit clingier to me lately—particularly when Mr. Dorsey was out of town—and I secretly wondered if once someone was given a bit of love, they missed it more when it was gone. It was certainly the case with Mama.

I obeyed Zoë's command and I increased my clip. Winnie shook her head in exhaustion, and Zoë further propped herself up on her saddle, as if she were involved in a secret equestrian show to which I was not privy. I hated tugging at Winnie's rope, but I gave it another nudge.

"Sorry, Winnie," I mumbled under my breath as I pulled her and Zoë forward.

Winnie sighed to indicate she understood it wasn't my fault.

"Mr. Dorsey comes home in three days," Zoë said. Zoë had been emotionally absent lately; it was almost as if only the shell of Zoë Christie was in Ix and the rest of her—the important parts—were in Santa Fe beside Mr. Dorsey.

"That's nice," I said, not knowing what response was expected.

"Yes, it's been extremely difficult to have him away for so long. I worry about him sometimes, as he tends to overwork."

I nodded. At school, Zoë would talk about Mr. Dorsey like he was her boyfriend. Other kids couldn't relate, but that didn't matter; they savored her every word as if each were a piece of candy from an expensive chocolate store. The subject of Mr. Dorsey seemed to cut off Zoë's sharp edges and make them rounder, nicer. Therefore I asked:

"What does he look like?"

"Mr. Dorsey is . . ." She paused to grab the right adjective from her limited repertoire. "Actually, he is perhaps the most beautiful man I've ever met in real life. His hair is blond but you can tell it will be gray soon. At one time it was curly, but now it isn't. Oh, and he cuts it himself. Once a week." Zoë seemed impressed by this fact, so impressed that she paused in her ramblings to once again consider it. "His eyes are blue. He confided in me that he's disappointed in their pantone, but I'm not. Mommy took me to Honolulu last year, and the water there is the exact color of Mr. Dorsey's eyes."

I nodded. I had never been to Honolulu, so such a comparison was a bit incomprehensible to me. A frog had hopped over from the fish pond, and he blocked our path on the riding ring. Zoë, unfortunately, noticed.

"We need to call an exterminator. The estate is being overrun by wildlife." She paused and veered back to the only subject which interested her. "The water in Hawaii is see-through blue, not cloudy blue like it is in the oceans here."

The frog hopped away and we continued forward.

Zoë continued, "Mr. Dorsey is tall, too, which is good for me because I am lanky." It was true, Zoë's limbs were like Winnie's. She was the tallest girl in our class, even without the spiky shoes she always wore to punctuate that fact. "Oh, and his body is perfect. He is very skinny but has muscles in his arms."

I nodded. Zoë had seen Mr. Dorsey's body. This could only mean one thing: Mr. Dorsey really was Zoë Christie's boyfriend.

Two weeks later, however, Mr. Dorsey returned from Santa Fe and something was very wrong. Although she still maintained her meticulously pressed and dry-cleaned veneer, there was something noticeably awry with the illustrious Zoë Christie. Others may not have noticed it, but I saw her through a very big make-up mirror. It wasn't as if Zoë Christie were outwardly blemished, but there was something wrong inside. Zoë spent hours gazing at her Modernist locker, yet now she tried to find in it faults. She deliberately forgot to water her orchid, but her surreptitious tears when the very flower began to die could have provided rain for an entire forest. In addition, the generally materially aware girl entered the wrong long black car one day and did not discover her snafu until she arrived at a nonarchitectural estate on the other side of the county and could not find Winnie in its stables.

Zoë was suffering from maladies of the heart, and she was even more aloof. Although I longed to see Winnie and the other creatures at Zoë's architectural estate, she rarely invited me now, and I did not press her on this issue.

"Oh my God. Oh my God. Oh my God."

Zoë was sprinting down the hall, out of a classroom. Her black spiky stilettos clanked on the linoleum floor. She wore a black ruffled dress, more suitable for France than French II. Heavy black eyeliner completed the look.

Zoë slumped over her locker and fiddled with the combination.

"Even his birth date is eluding me."

Zoë said this with exasperation as she maniacally tugged at the padlock.

"What?" I asked.

"Mr. Dorsey's birth date, my locker combination."

Apparently, these were one and the same.

"Is everything okay?" I asked.

"No. Everything is the furthest from okay."

Then, in an instant, Zoë Christie remembered something. She was Zoë Christie. She once again put on her Zoë Christie mask. It was calm, serene, aloof, with unsmeared black eyeliner and million-dollar red lipstick.

She breathed exaggeratedly and her red, short fingernails caressed the padlock.

"Five. Six . . ."

Zoë faded out before she reached the last number—presumably the year of birth—and the locker miraculously opened. The orchid had been propped up with a number of twigs; brown sticks were trying to save the erotic flower.

I arrived at Zoë Christie's architectural estate with dread. Zoë had demanded I bring *Dorsey: The Unfinished Works* so she could do research into Mr. Dorsey's past; a past which she was convinced was hindering her future. As expected, however, Kris Tina Woo refused to relinquish the book if only for a minute, and she resorted to locking the text with a heavy chain lest I consider taking it without her permission.

Zoë's temper could be volatile—this I knew—and worst case scenarios floated through my mind. One can always tell a woman's true character in how she treats the servants, Mrs. Christie would say to her furniture, and by such count Zoë Christie was a woman of little character. If I was honest with myself, I was a servant to Zoë: There was something expected of me, and I could not deliver. Although one of her better traits had always been her eerily calm façade, the teen had still been emotionally wayward at school. She was locker-obsessed, but her relationship with her single white orchid was a fickle one. Zoë would complain about the flower's hue, its posture. Is an orchid even Modernist? Zoë Christie would ask her sleek mirror, but then minutes later she would gaze at the orchid as if it were a flower in her wedding bouquet.

At the architectural estate, Zoë's governess escorted me to the stables. Winnie whinnied and seemed genuinely happy to see me. She tossed her head back exaggeratedly (I long suspected this was a habit she had acquired from Zoë) and motioned for me to come closer. I picked up a wooden brush and looked around. I was alone.

"Hi, there, Winnie. It's so good to see you," I said. "I've missed you very much."

She smiled, and she offered me her leg.

"An itch?"

She nodded, and I began to brush her.

"Did Zoë ride you this morning?" I asked. Winnie wore her expensive leather saddle that Zoë's daddy had brought her back from a business trip to Paris. The saddle's oversized orange box still sat at the foot of Zoë's bed and functioned as a place for the girl to throw dirty clothing for the maids.

Winnie nodded and motioned for me to brush her brown fluffy mane. She wiggled uncomfortably under the weight of the saddle.

"Where is Le Cheval?" I asked. Le Cheval was Winnie's best friend.

Winnie whinnied, blushed, batted her long eyelashes, and pointed to the adjacent Altman Estate with her hoof. The estate was not architectural (I couldn't tell the difference, but Zoë had informed me of this fact a few dozen times), yet it was multi-acred and beautiful. Le Cheval's stable was roughly the size of my house.

Suddenly I heard shoes on dirt, boots on hay. Two sets of feet were coming closer. I heard Zoë's quiet voice first.

"Winnie is one of my most prized possessions. Besides my new jud desk, of course." Zoë paused here, for an effect I did not understand. Her companion did not respond. "Winnie is a thoroughbred.

She will eventually be a champion thoroughbred, but not yet because she is too young."

There was still no response from Zoë's companion, but it soon became clear the couple was heading closer so that Zoë could show this person her future champion thoroughbred. I knew Zoë would be embarrassed of me and get angry if I were seen, so I jumped into a stack of hay in the stable. "This is Winnie." Zoë giggled a little. It was the first time she ever sounded humble or even insecure. "Winnie, this is Mr. Dorsey."

She said this facetiously, as if Winnie could not really understand who she was meeting.

"Hello, Winnie."

The voice was baritone and beautiful and even a bit . . . unsure. I held my breath as he continued, "She is much more beautiful than a piece of furniture."

"Yes, well, perhaps. But she is not as dear to me because you didn't pick her out." Zoë said this with admiration, and I could tell that she was glaring meanly at Winnie. She did this often, if the horse missed a particularly tall jump or broke her stride. "Although I'm a very proficient rider, I intend to send Winnie to a proper jockey so she can be in derbies."

Winnie was going to be sent away?

"What a shame," Mr. Dorsey said, as if articulating my very thoughts.

"I only want to do what's best for Winnie, of course." Zoë paused as she said this. I read the insincerity of the comment and hoped Mr. Dorsey did, too. Zoë continued, "Perhaps we shall go back to the main house. For all their style, jodhpurs can be terribly uncomfortable."

The last sentence was soaked in flirtation. Mr. Dorsey, however, remained detached.

"That's a good idea, actually. I should really talk to your mother about the lowey chest I intend to put in the third bedroom."

"Of course. A lowey chest is exactly what that room needs."

Zoë's voice reeked of disappointment and, for the first time, I felt sorry for her. As they walked away, I pulled myself out of the haystack and looked around. The stables, Winnie, the green acres of perfectly groomed grass, the impressive angles of the architectural estate: all this beauty suddenly seemed very lonely. Mr. Dorsey's affection was the only thing the Christies couldn't afford to buy their daughter, and unfortunately it was the only thing she wanted.

Mr. Dorsey had departed the architectural estate, and Zoë's governess informed me I was to leave as well.

Due to scheduling conflicts with the driver, Mrs. Christie was to be the one to take me home to Unity, but she was notoriously late and today was no exception. She left me standing on the driveway for close to an hour. Darkness descending on the estate.

Out of boredom, I wandered over to the fish pond. Although the family often forgot its existence, the Christies' pond was one of my favorite parts of the estate. Despite its repeated cleanings, the man-made swamp was green and mildewed. A heavy layer of slime often covered its surface. I liked this because it reminded me that somehow nature always wins, even against a team of servants and potent liquid cleaners. I leaned toward the dirty water. A crawfish swam nervously as a baby minnow darted in her new surroundings. Two swordfish pretended to be engaged in a heated fencing battle. I suspected the Christies would send their chef to catch dinner from the pond, and I looked at shrimp and tuna and lobsters and wished I could take them home with me in a giant net. They did not deserve to be eaten, even by the illustrious Christies.

Unbeknownst to me, Mrs. Christie stood behind me as I pet a little crab.

"Does this look like the driveway?" This was one of Mrs. Christie's better quips.

"No, Mrs. Christie. I apologize." The little crab shrunk away from us, probably afraid of being eaten. "I just love the fish pond and wanted to say good-bye to the fish." I had a strong feeling this was to be my last visit to the architectural estate.

"My, you are a strange girl."

I just nodded.

"Your poor mother," Mrs. Christie continued.

I did not know to which meaning Mrs. Christie was referring—either your mother has her hands full or I heard your mother's crazy—so I again merely nodded. The sun was setting, and I wondered if the Christies took this all for granted. Perhaps proprietors of equestrian estates eventually tired of purple skies, maybe they even complained about the golden sun setting behind the stable night after night.

My backpack sat beside me, but Mrs. Christie did not seem in a hurry to leave. Instead, she hovered.

"I worry about Zoë sometimes," she finally said, and my eyes followed hers to the riding ring. Zoë held Winnie behind her on a long brown leather rope. She hadn't yet slipped out of her uncomfortable jodhpurs, and she wore with them a felt riding cap and knee-length riding boots. The ring was far away, and for the first time, Zoë looked very small in her vast surroundings. "Occasionally I wonder if all this"—Mrs. Christie swept her diamond-bangled arm into the estate's horizon—"keeps her from understanding that life brings with it sadness."

I could not think of anything to say. But I suddenly wanted desperately to have a mom back.

It was silent for a moment as we looked at Zoë. Lap after lap, Zoë and Winnie made the same circle; it was almost as if it were an exercise in discipline.

"He was wrong for her." Mrs. Christie looked very sad now, as if Zoë's broken heart had been miraculously transplanted in her. "He's thirty-four, she's seventeen. Certainly she's lovely, but he never once looked at her. It was only a one-sided love. Which can't be love."

Sun, light, darkness, moon, stars, clouds all fought for their position in the sky, but it was crowded, and I knew that soon darkness would win.

"She's always been sophisticated for her age. But, well, I wish she weren't in such a hurry to grow up." Mrs. Christie looked at me, then Zoë. Zoë was still walking Winnie around the ring, oblivious to darkness. "He's odd, really."

It took me a moment to understand that she was referring to Mr. Dorsey. The creatures in the pond hovered at the water's surface. They must have wanted to see the sky or maybe they felt sad, too. The water bubbled with their breath, but Mrs. Christie didn't seem to hear.

"He disappears sometimes. Nobody knows where he goes. It's almost as if . . ." Mrs. Christie looked to the sky, and a flash of recognition that she was seeing something magnificent seemed to register, but just as quickly it was gone. "It's almost as if he fades away, turns into a ghost."

Mrs. Christie was giving me time to respond, but I did not know what to say. I looked at one of the stars—a really bright one—and I wished for a mom.

"Zorka." Mrs. Christie paused here, and she almost looked scared at what she was about to say. "Never fall in love with a ghost."

Darkness was overwhelming light, stars pushed away the sun, and Mrs. Christie fingered one of her diamond bracelets. I knew little about love, but I could tell by looking at her that Mrs. Christie had once fallen in love with a tortured soul as Zoë and Mama had. I was not going to make that mistake, too. I was sad enough.

Mrs. Christie motioned to my backpack with her eyes, cueing our departure. I looked down at the fish pond one last time. A tuna swam to the surface, and I could tell he did not want me to go away because he feared it would be forever. I blew him a kiss, picked up my bag, and looked to the riding ring one last time.

Winnie was tied to an old oak tree. The estate was gated, but Zoë must have forgotten this; once one thing escapes you, I think it is human nature to tie everything closer lest they walk away. This was a lesson I had learned a long time ago—I had spent years watching Mama try to tie Daddy closer with her love—but Zoë Christie was just learning this lesson now, in the form of Mr. Dorsey. Zoë wandered around the ring a few times. She picked a stray wildflower, adjusted a jump height, swatted at a buzzing mosquito.

Finally, she looked around, sat down on the dirt, and began to cry.

Without warning, graduation loomed nearer. Inflated words like future and college floated through the halls. College had never been a reality in the Carpenter family, but I desperately wanted to leave Unity. I wanted to go to a school where people would like me, where I could have friends.

I never told anyone this, but Mrs. Pascal—my science teacher—seemed to understand. She stopped by unannounced; I was ashamed of our rickety house, of Mama's lavender robe with cigarette burns, of the screen door that still sat on the porch. When I saw her standing beside the doorbell, I thought briefly about Zoë's architectural estate, and I wished I lived in a house that was like falling water. But Mrs. Pascal didn't notice. She walked into the foyer and commented on the nice picture on the wall. It was a photograph of Daddy and me; Mama had taken it many years ago, when my hair was so light it was white. A butterfly had landed on my shoulder and I was giggling. Daddy, on the other hand, was staring past the camera at something I couldn't see. His expression was blank.

"That's one of my favorite photographs of Zorka."

Mrs. Pascal and I turned to Mama. I excused myself to the kitchen and poured Mrs. Pascal some ice water in an old wineglass. It was chipped a little at the edges, and I hoped she wouldn't notice. She thanked me, ignoring the chips.

"It's such a pleasure to meet you," Mrs. Pascal began. She stared right into Mama's eyes. They were crazy eyes now, but Mrs. Pascal did not appear to notice this either, though she was generally so perceptive.

"It's nice to meet you, too," Mama responded. "Do you work at Zorka's school?"

Mrs. Pascal nodded. I sat down in Daddy's old armchair. A stray brush rabbit had hopped into the house earlier, and I caressed her back. The shy, elusive brush rabbits generally only travel short distances, and this entrance into public domain was extremely unusual.

"I am sorry to barge in like this," began Mrs. Pascal. "But Zorka is so humble I knew she would never allow for a meeting in her honor."

Mama smiled, as if the compliment were meant for her.

Mrs. Pascal continued, "I am here to discuss Zorka's future. As you most likely are aware, Zorka wants to be a veterinarian. We expect her to graduate in the top of the class. This is a tremendous honor and an indication of future success. With this in mind, I have taken the liberty of applying for a number of science scholarships for Zorka in order that she may attend a university."

The brush rabbit's ears perked high at this unexpected nibble of information.

"I see." Mama's response was accompanied by a quick nod of the head as she fiddled with a burn hole in her bathrobe. "I would be very honored for Zorka to attend college."

I smiled, and Mrs. Pascal couched her grin with a slight nod.

"Here are the scholarship acceptance forms," Mrs. Pascal said and pulled them from her leather briefcase. They were well ordered, with colored individual tabs that said "Sign Here." "If you would, please sign where indicated." Mrs. Pascal provided a fountain pen. The rabbit hopped beside me on the chair's arm.

Mama slowly opened the papers; the crinkle was loud. The rabbit stopped, alarmed at the sudden commotion. Mrs. Pascal leaned forward, pen in hand.

There was a long pause. "I will have to run these by our lawyer," said Mama.

"I can assure you, this is just a formality. The forms are quite standard," Mrs. Pascal began.

I looked closely at the brush rabbit's erect ears. Rabbits who lived in hot inland regions tended to have longer ears than those living on the cooler, humid northern coast. Presumably this was because sound did not travel as well in hot, dry air as in moist, cool air, so rabbits in these climates needed to pick up sounds more effectively.

My future was in the hands of an attorney who only existed in Mama's mind.

D r. Cossman was the dork in high school—the kid with zits, chunky glasses, and an in-depth knowledge of the periodic table—who somehow became cool around his mid-forties. Dr. Cossman's Cactusarium was established to little fanfare; its founder, the illustrious Dr. Cossman himself, was a self-proclaimed fanatic of the prickly species, and his dedication to studying, probing, and researching the plants had virtually thrown him into bankruptcy. But twenty-two years after he started, Dr. Cossman stumbled across a genetic defect in the *Ariocarpus* cactus that enabled the plant to produce a fiery substance when it incestuously mated with the *Pelecyphora strobiliformis*. The resulting gene mutation, called Cossfixer by its modest founder, was lauded for its anti-aging effects and, despite FDA warnings, was smuggled into dermatologists' office throughout the States. Grants ensued, Dr. Cossman made multimillions, and the cacti park was now world renowned. Dr. Cossman's Cactusarium had arrived, fashionably late.

I, on the other hand, arrived unfashionably early. The butterfly who had flown around in my stomach during the ride procreated the moment I entered the park. It was immediately evident that my button-down dress was precisely wrong for the occasion. I hoped Dr. Cossman would not take my poor choice of attire into account when he made his hiring selection. I desperately wanted to be a cacti caretaker; I felt as if the bedside manner and biological acumen that would have suited me well in the veterinary world would be readily transferable to plants. And of all plants, cacti were my favorite species, as they—like me—demanded lots of sunlight, little water, and had big spikes to keep unwanted people away.

I had been waiting for sixteen minutes when Dr. Cossman finally summoned me into the converted janitor's closet he called an office. Cossman was gray-haired and his white doctor's coat had "Doctor Alfred Cossman" stitched in a dark hue of maroon. The protractor, bullet-shaped burgundy pen, and scientific calculator that filled this pocket would have suggested Cossman held a doctorate in engineering or medicine rather than botany. Something told me this false impression was intentional.

The world-renowned doctor was on the phone negotiating a complicated transaction involving a sea urchin cactus and an illegal drug of some sort when I entered the closet. World wars had been settled more quickly.

"Why, hello there," Dr. Cossman said. His self-importance was communicable. We sat eye-to-eye, but I felt as if he were standing on a conductor's platform while I was crouched in an orchestra pit.

"Hi, Dr. Cossman," I began. His handshake felt like a salmon trying to squirm his way out of a net. Even the office was starting to reek of rancid fish. I stifled the smell and quickly continued. "It's such a pleasure to meet you. I'm a huge fan of your work."

"Well, thank you. That goes without saying," Cossman answered before perusing a photocopy of my high school transcript. He looked at me with the deep and intent eyes of a chess player.

I diverted my stare to a photograph of the infamous doctor shaking hands with a dignitary. Cossman caught this, threw me a slight smirk, and refocused on the nearly blemish-free transcript.

"Hmmm. Grades are okay, not up to our typical standards, though. What is this? An A minus in AP English? We really need people here to be able to communicate with the cacti, if you see what I mean. This A minus is very worrisome," Cossman continued.

To my untrained mind, holding a watering can and analyzing Tolstoy were not exactly related.

"Yes, sir, I understand that A minus is of concern. You see, my thesis on *Anna Karenina* as an embodiment of prerevolutionist Russia was perhaps a little weak. Is Russian prewar literature something your cacti are interested in? If so, I regrettably may not be the right candidate for the job, for my Tolstoy knowledge only encapsulates his earlier works," I said matter of factly.

This false modesty knocked Dr. Cossman off his game plan, ever so slightly.

"Well, I'm impressed you're admitting your weaknesses," Cossman said. "It takes a brave person to do that. Actually, Russian literature does happen to be of particular interest to a number of the species, but I think perhaps we can overlook your little Tolstoy hiccup."

I was convinced this man could not even spell Tolstoy, but I played along.

"I do have a very extensive knowledge of South American literature, as well as of twentieth-century American and European literature," I responded. I paused, then switched tactics. "Incidentally, I happened to notice *Scapharostrus* when I walked in. What a beautiful example of a living rock cactus. . . . I've never seen that species so large and with such poise. You must have paid him special care in his upbringing."

Intellect and flattery went a long way, particularly in combination.

"Yes, he is quite beautiful, isn't he? All of my cacti are, however. I look forward to showing you the collection."

"And when will you be doing that, sir?" I asked, knowing the response.

"Your first day of work, of course. You're hired."

"That's terrific!" I responded, with a touch of rah-rah. I hoped to put a punctuation point on this meeting.

My wish was the phone's command. Cossman picked it up, third ring, and I took its cue.

VIII

Mama was very sick.

In the beginning, I had assumed that she would get better. I thought Sister Jean and Pastor Bob would find the right hospital for her, and she would walk home one day with a new daddy on her arm and my life would go back to normal. Seven years after Daddy left, though, I sat alone on my birthday. Mama was at a prayer group. Statues of St. Jude, the patron saint of hopeless causes, now covered our house.

I picked up a single chocolate cupcake, sitting alone on the kitchen table. I sang "Happy Birthday" to myself quietly—"Happy Birthday, dear Zorka"—and lit candles. They burned bright, but I could not find for them a wish. I knew Mama was never getting better. The future seemed sad, the saddest it had ever seemed.

I found Mama lying on the edge of the bed, wearing her wedding gown.

It did not fit her anymore, not because she had put on weight around the middle—like women were supposed to when they aged and had babies, settling into midlife stability—but because she was starving herself to death. Bones poked through the jaundiced antique lace. It was the first time in years I had seen Mama in makeup, but her blue eyeshadow and red lipstick looked as if they belonged on a sad clown or in a nursery school finger-painting class. Mama's crown of blond hair, once molded into beehives and French twists, was matted into a web of grease and tangles. Pearl earrings weighted down her ears, dark circles weighted down her eyes, and off-color satin pumps should have lifted her feet two inches off the floor.

A cracked hand mirror sat on the bed.

Although doctors threw around terms such as "coma" and "unconscious," Mama looked like she was in a long sleep. She was a skeleton, and even when I dialed 911, I could not help but think she looked kind of like an animal whose source of food had gone extinct.

I talked to Mama as the sirens of the ambulance turned the corner of Honey Creek Parkway and continued speaking to her at the hospital. I guess I thought perhaps my speech would wake her up, keep her alive, convince death that she had something to live for.

I thought I had won temporary reprieve from death when Mama awoke at the hospital. A clear plastic freezer bag supplied her with food that looked like water, clear plastic tubes breathed for her, and a complicated-looking machine informed me, through a series of beeps and green zigzags, that Mama was still alive. Doctors checked clipboarded items, nurses scurried, Mama rested, and I chattered, "Mama, there's a sale at the department store now; fifty percent off all merchandise. There was a black dress that would look great on you. It had one of those collars—you know, the ones with the really low necks . . ."

"Cowl neck, sweetheart. A cowl neck."

"That's right, a cowl neck," I said, kissing her forehead. "How are

Read too many books like this and you're going to wind up in La La Land!

M.

:all the ambulance, but I didn't know
ome soon."

wore a cowl neck sweater the night of
he fell in love with me the moment I

kly?" I asked. Usually I did not men-
onged for Mama's voice. Besides, love
about.

nk the truest loves often do," Mama

er person?" I asked.

eetheart," Mama began. "It may be
ir cologne or their breath or their af-
tershave, but a smell which you don't even know exists—or it may be the way they move their hips, or the way they look at a single blade of grass. But, whatever it is, you will never know it. Your heart will know, but your mind won't. And you can spend years trying to figure it out, but you never will."

"What if no one ever falls in love with me?"

"Oh, many men will fall in love with you, Zorka. The bigger question is which man will you fall in love with."

"What do you think he'll be like?"

"That's a very good question. If I had to guess, I bet he'll be really smart—like you—and have a vivid imagination. And I hope he'll be kind, because that's the most important thing."

"But what if he doesn't love me back? How do you fall out of love?"

"That's the part I haven't figured out yet," Mama answered candidly.

She closed her eyes. The machine with the green line shrieked continuously and the screech was off-pitch and hurt my ears and must have been heard in the nurses' lounge, for they soon hovered over Mama like vultures. The stark white room was hazy, and for the first time I felt as if I were looking at a life through glass. I did not know whose life this was, a poor girl whose father abandoned her, whose mother died, who no one had ever understood.

Even in death, Mama waited patiently for Daddy. She was buried in Ix, between Grandmother Zorka and a small rectangular piece of grass that should have covered Daddy's remains. Only I assumed Daddy was somewhere far away, and would probably be buried in a crypt with his in-laws and new children, maybe even in a double-coffin holding hands with his new wife. People have lived months, years, decades even, with hope. I suppose Mama believed hope could last even longer in death.

Mama's funeral was a service for thirteen. In addition to Pastor Bob and me, attendees included Zoë and Mrs. Christie (it seemed the polite thing to do), Todd Sunday, Sister Jean, Mr. Ritter (of the funeral home), and six pallbearers. I probably should not count the pallbearers, since they were for-hire and paid by Mr. Ritter on a per funeral basis, but I will anyway. Mama would have been impressed by the attendance, particularly as Ix was an hour drive away, and a nasty cold front followed her death.

I remember little of the funeral itself. I vaguely recall Pastor Bob's affectionate words, Mama's new wooden home being lowered into an open hole, the faraway tintinnabulation of church bells. I carried a small bouquet of lavender, and I recall the flowers' pungency. I recall Todd Sunday's brief eulogy, a short speech revolving around Mama's following at the supermarket, and I remember wondering how long

Mama would even stay a body and what her soul looked like. When Pastor Bob blessed Mama for the final time, I remember thinking that I hoped all that prayer had paid off for Mama. I wondered if she was in Heaven looking down at me, looking at God, or looking at Daddy. Maybe God would have some sort of filter so she would not have to see him with his new wife. Heaven didn't seem the place for broken hearts.

Oddly enough, what I remember most about the funeral was Zoë. She was radiant, in a real fur coat with matching hat and little black heels. She fidgeted a lot throughout the ceremony; at first I thought this was because she was embarrassed, but then I figured out it was because her delicate heels were sinking into the wet, sloppy grass. Her hair was blond and flipped out from under her hat, her eyes were glassy but not teary. Once during the ceremony she smiled at me—it was a smirk really—and I grinned toothily in response. She looked down and nudged her mom. Her mother looked at her, then me.

I held my lavender when Zoë sauntered up behind me. She walked like a ballerina and had acquired a slight accent with which to affect her wispy voice. She always sounded as if she was out of breath now. Perhaps she was. Maybe being so perfect demanded a lot of effort.

"I didn't know your mother's middle name was Jane," she said. She could not disguise her indifference, but I forgave her. My innate ability to forgive was acquired from Mama.

"Yes, Catherine Jane," I said. I examined the lavender. "Is that coat real fur?"

"Yes. Daddy has a mink farm now. It's a side project. He gets really stressed at work, you know, so hobbies calm him down."

Zoë showed me her collar. A real face stared back at me. He was weaselly looking, with little fangs and closed eyes. A beautiful specimen. I could not imagine that anyone, let alone my former best friend, would walk around with a deceased creature around her neck. I forgave her again, though. "Daddy left his head so I would see how mean he was and not feel guilty about wearing him."

"How does a mink farm work?" I asked.

"I don't know the intricacies of the operation. But I think Daddy raises minks in little cages and kills them when they're just babies. Six months or something. He keeps the best females and a few males to breed for future years."

"Oh. Isn't he sad? Killing innocent creatures like that?"

"No, he raises them to die. If it wasn't for my Daddy, they wouldn't be born in the first place." Zoë opened her jacket once again and petted the lining, as if it were still a living, breathing mink. "Would you like to try it on? See, even the lining is tied together with grosgrain ribbon." Sure enough, perfectly knotted little brown bows tied animal to cloth.

"No, thank you," I answered.

A pause hung in the air, lingering just long enough to become a memory.

"My boyfriend and I just broke up, so I kind of know what your Mama was going through," Zoë began. Zoë had a boyfriend? "I am really sorry about everything."

"Everything meaning my mother or our friendship?" I asked in uncharacteristic boldness.

"I meant your Mama, but I guess both." Zoë started to pick absently at my lavender. We both stood for a moment, and I grew light-headed.

Lavender petals fell to the ground, slowly, like paper airplanes on a windy day.

When I looked up, Zoë was already gone. She was on her way to her mommy's fancy sports car, to her daddy's latest side project, to her friends. Zoë was pretty and had boyfriends and coats tied with grosgrain. I looked down at Mama's coffin. They had not put the dirt over it yet, and I wanted to bring it home with me. At least I wouldn't have to be alone.

I heard the British motor of Zoë's sleek car and could almost feel its exhaust as it drove away. As I looked down at the bare stem in my hand, I could not help but think that perhaps the world was one giant mink farm, and we were all just being raised to die.

The forest was particularly vibrant. A speedy bobcat dashed through the dense undergrowth and raced a red fox for a tatter of dead raccoon. Ludic squirrels played with walnuts and each other. A pronghorn stretched long and lazy, absently observing shrews playing in a nearby copse. He was disinterested, however, full from a meal, and scratching his antlers. Did antlers have feeling, I wondered? I would research this when I returned home. A buck protected his doe who protected her fawn, and the veery bird was particularly talkative, chattering with other birds in tones of melody. Crickets talked back, angry at the clouds that hid the stars. A coyote tended to an injured member of his species, and my marvel at this phenomenon stretched from minutes to hours. How did animals understand what humans could not?

I finally returned home close to midnight, red-eyed and tired. I changed into my nightgown and briefly debated: Should I retire for the evening, or research the antler and its nerve activity?

I decided on the former, as there was no need for animal investigation anymore. Such pastimes were for veterinarians, not Zorka Carpenter.

I walked to the lamp to turn it off, but it darkened two seconds ahead of my step. The bulb sizzled with flair, then went black.

"Only the male pronghorn has antlers, and the horns are predominantly used in mating rituals." The voice was low, but still had a touch of whimsy. Although the content of the sentence could have been called scientific, the tone lacked exactitude.

I scanned the room. I was alone.

Minutes passed, but the eerie feeling did not. I got out of bed, and I skimmed my animal library, eventually deciding on a thickly bound book entitled *Pronghorns and Their Horn Structures*. As could be expected, the specific antler research was not elusive: "Only the male pronghorn has antlers, and the horns are predominantly used in mating rituals."

Perhaps I had read this fact before, I told—no, convinced—myself. Certainly, I had absorbed enough detail about pronghorns in my day; the prior February I had become obsessed with the creatures, roaming the forests with binoculars and befriending a few of the specimens.

I lay down again and rested my head on my pillow.

"You didn't have to check up on me. A few of my best friends have antlers."

The voice sounded close.

"Who are you?" I implored. Was I going crazy like Mama?

His giggle was low and mischievous. "I came in with you from the forest. It looked like you could use some cheering up. This bedroom's a mess, by the way. I'm going to get to work on cleaning it tomorrow."

I looked toward the general area of the voice. A little termite—the size of a pin's head cubed, perhaps—looked at me with bulbous eyes and what, I sensed, was a smile.

"Is this you?" I asked.

"For someone who claims to know so much about animals, you sure are clueless sometimes," was his caustic retort.

A small handful of seconds later, the termite hopped away. I looked at my bare shoulder, down my nightgown, in my pillowcases, through my sheets.

He was gone.

X

I ran into Kris Tina Woo in Hal's Hardware.

The Princeton School of Architecture had groomed her into the young architect she had always hoped to become; her hair was molded into a bouffant held precariously by rulers, her clothes were neatly tailored and in shades of white. She was still carrying her blue architecture book, of course, but it now peeked from a canvas messenger bag full of rolled-up blueprints. Kris Tina's attitude was soaked in impatience, but it was the good kind, the kind that implied she had someplace important to be.

Despite Princeton's cherry-on-top touches, however, I recognized Kris Tina immediately. She was ahead of me in line buying an X-acto knife, extra sharp #2 pencils, and a protractor. I was purchasing a new goldfish bowl—Flounder had outgrown his. Kris Tina still had a ruler behind her ear, and she strutted with the air of someone who designed things that would last a long time.

"Well, hello there, Zorka," Kris Tina said, glancing at the bowl. "Is that a goldfish bowl you're buying?"

"It is. How's Princeton?" I asked. I hoped jealousy did not find its way into my tone, but I suspected it did.

"Why, thank you for remembering. It's spectacular. Do you mind if I look at that bowl for a moment?" she asked with intention.

"Feel free," I responded. "It's just a goldfish bowl."

"That's precisely what I am afraid of." Kris Tina cupped the bowl in her hands and examined it closely. "I regret to inform you that this model is not ergonomically correct." This was her final verdict.

"It's just a bowl for my Flounder," I answered.

"Your Flounder lives in this?" she asked with amazement.

"Yes. I am afraid so. I don't have access to a fish pond."

"I see." Kris Tina pulled her ruler from her ear, placed it on her checkbook, and wrote out the check for Hal. I watched her quietly. The perfect, square letters could have come from a typewriter. Kris Tina so adored her calling that even a number was a work of art.

"I think I may have both long- and short-term solutions to your problem," Kris Tina finally responded, after she had mulled a problem I did not even know I had. "Which one would you like me to present first?"

"Short, please," I said. Long seemed too far away.

"As you wish. Das Haus Retro, are you familiar with it?" She didn't allow me time to answer. "I don't suspect you are." She handed me a business card; words were handwritten in pencil and the penmanship resembled Kris Tina's. "It is a by-recommendation-only store. Tell Mr. Hamilton that I suggested you see him. His fish bowls are designed by architects and engineers who understand oxygen intake, algae, and their applications to the fish habitat. In addition, from a design perspective, the bowls work seamlessly with an end table, a coffee table, even a kitchen table, if you so desire."

"Oh," I said. This was the only response I could formulate in two seconds. I wished I had a tape recorder so I could play back Kris Tina's response in slow motion.

"As for the long-term solution," she began with mischief in her eye. "Do you have a car?"

Rumors of Woo Case Study House #1's existence had flitted about for over a year, but I had never cared to confirm them. A few times I had contemplated visiting the structure, yet something had always held me back. I don't know what that something was, but I suspect it fell somewhere in that triangle with envy, apathy, and self-absorption as its points. Surely, the townsfolk were proud of Kris Tina and her incredible accomplishment; the house was a bastion for local photographers and was said to have been pictured on the cover of Princeton's application ("Princeton Architecture School: Every angle can be transparent").

Sure enough, rumors were confirmed. If Kris Tina's goal had been to make something complex look simple, she had succeeded marvelously. Woo Case Study House #1 was a massive and rectangular indoor-outdoor greenhouse, a glass structure which would unite nature and home living. Its only nonglass supports came in the form of aluminum rods which connected the massive sheets of ceiling glass. Despite its many vectors, the structure somehow managed to look streamlined. Kris Tina, who cited Eastern European Modernists as her influences, was concerned with the structure's well-being when she went back to Princeton. After all, New Jersey was really far away.

She had considered hiring a caretaker, but she wanted someone to fully experience the Case Study House and report the results to her. This would help strengthen her thesis, she explained, and would maybe even make her more valuable to a big name firm someday (she was already priceless because she was a female Modernist, and those are rare, she made point to mention).

Kris Tina put the ruler to the air, as she had long ago with Dorsey Monument One, and mumbled something about decimeters and the sun.

"Is that a rogue prism on the ceiling?" I pointed toward an imaginary error.

"Coincidental you should ask, because the answer is no." Kris Tina paused. "Zorka, as you may be aware, I am going to be traveling around the world before I return to Princeton for winter semester."

"I wasn't aware."

"That is quite odd. The town is abuzz with discussion of my upcoming travels." Kris Tina pulled out her binoculars. "I will be visiting Beijing, Iceland, Oslo, Belize, Cape Town, Riyadh, Iran, and . . ." She faded out here.

I looked to Woo Case Study House #1 and was almost blinded by the sun's reflection on its angles. While I toiled away at the Cactusarium, Kris Tina Woo was personally going to experience Dorsey Monuments One through Nine.

". . . well, I am not aware of my final destination. But I am determined to find Architect Dorsey's residence, and interview its client for my thesis." Kris Tina paused then continued. "Unlike lesser universities, Princeton is a proponent of the hands-on approach and thus requires its students to complete a Case Study House before graduation. I completed mine early, in order to travel to Architect Dorsey's monuments," the portentous architecture student explained, and she looked at her blue text. "There is only so much you can learn from books."

Kris Tina opened the glass door.

Case studies were not perfect specimens, even in Kris Tina's admission, but I liked this. I had been collecting creatures for three years now, and mine were not flawless specimens either. Termite was a workaholic, Ladybug had no spots. Worm did not squiggle quite right, Centipede had only ninety-nine legs, Firefly glowed only ten watts, Snail always walked at forty-five miles per hour, Catfish did not have whiskers. Nightingale had been born without a voice, Goldfish was not gold, and Tarantula tended to get attached too easily. Perfect specimens belonged to perfect lives, not to Zorka Carpenter. I took great care in discovering new members of my family. I found many of my creatures in nearby ponds and fields and trees; some were friends of my current creatures, others would knock on my door late at night.

Three days after my first introduction to Woo Case Study House #1, my 310 creatures accompanied me to the greenhouse. As I had suspected, it was love. My land creatures crawled, danced, and played ring-around-the-rosy on the shiny cement floor. My air creatures flitted about, enjoying their newfound freedom and unrestricted views, playing in the greenhouse's trees, plants, and ferns. At one point I was afraid Chameleon was permanently lost in the foliage. My water creatures, whose abodes previously consisted of little fish bowls (ergonomically incorrect ones, it turned out) and the bathroom sinks, did back flips into the giant fish pond.

It was two hours before my creatures began to tire. Kris Tina escorted me to the area that would be my bedroom. It was all glass, as would be expected, and I almost felt as if I were standing in a kind, loving forest. A little white cot was the room's only furnishing. I imagined falling asleep here, night after night.

"Despite its diminutive proportions, I consider this room the architectural focus of the house." Kris Tina's tone was buoyant and sure. "I am certain you will discover this as well."

Kris Tina and I paused. My creatures had fallen into their afternoon naps. Woo Case Study House #1 was the ideal milieu for them; although my bedroom was small and barren, the creatures would be merely a thin sheet of glass from their natural environs. I glanced at Kris Tina. She was focused, too. She cranked open one of the windows slightly and adjusted a piece of seaweed in the pond. She turned to depart and handed me the keys to the Case Study.

"You have to fidget with them a little," she said. "My class on designing doors comes next year."

She paused.

"Zorka," Kris Tina commanded.

"Yes?"

"Your report should be double-spaced, typed in Franklin Gothic font," she said. "And feel free to include the part about the bedroom as the architectural heart of the home. You can take the quote directly; no need to footnote it or attribute it to the architect."

The ceiling began to leak as Kris Tina Woo closed the door behind her.

I moved into Woo Case Study House #1 one week later.

At first I worried the move would be traumatic. Not only was the relocation a logistical nightmare, as one might expect for a family of 310, but Mama's house was the final facet of my life which was tied to Daddy and the unit we had once called family. But as I packed up, I could envision Mama's support, even in Heaven. Before her heart had broken, she used to say I was destined for great things. I could not achieve greatness from a basement.

The Case Study House came with specific directions for cleaning and maintenance, and all pointed to Das Haus Retro. Since my rendezvous with Kris Tina in Hal's, I had had neither the time nor energy to make the hour-long drive to the mysterious storefront, but dust began to accumulate on the glass ("Windex simply will not do!" Kris Tina had exclaimed) and a thin sheet of vapor hovered around the ceiling when the weather was warm. And I still needed an ergonomically correct carrying bowl for my fish as, despite their new pond, they still enjoyed accompanying me on routine errands.

I assumed Das Haus Retro was the glassy building that rested on a hilltop halfway between Unity and the big city. There was no sign, no telltale evidence this was indeed the store. I glanced at Kris Tina's map—a piece of art so beautiful it could have been sold at auction—then at the building. Only two cars sat in the parking lot and both were parked crookedly over multiple spaces, as if their owners were simply too busy to pay heed to such trivialities as yellow lines. Kris Tina would have gone sleepless over such a faux pas.

Mr. Hamilton was a wiry-looking fellow whose pasty flesh hung off him like silk on a coat hanger. He swayed about with a confidence that was most likely restricted to his very limited domain. My creatures shifted uneasily in my purse. I wondered if Das Haus Retro had a mail-order catalogue.

"May I help you?" Hamilton asked condescendingly. His German accent was a welcome visitor that would occasionally penetrate his speech. Hamilton probably felt his native tongue unified him with the designers he and Kris Tina so admired.

"I am here on recommendation of Kris Tina Woo."

"She will be a very good Modernist someday." Hamilton's tone indicated his was the last word on the subject.

"I just moved into Woo Case Study House #1," I began. This was my only opportunity to name-drop, and I decided to maximize it. "I am in need of some cleaning supplies. Oh, and an ergonomically correct goldfish bowl."

"Let us take care of the goldfish bowl first," Hamilton said, as he whisked me to aisle one. "This is the only one I would ever recommend to my clients."

The white plastic bowl had a small glass peephole. It looked more like a smoke alarm than a fish bowl.

"It doesn't look as if it has much glass space," I said, examining it. My purse wiggled.

"Would you rather have a fish with open lungs or a good view?" he said acidly. I guess no one of my lowly caliber had ever disagreed with him on matters of design. "Besides, this is much more aesthetically pleasing to the eye than the traditional."

"That's valid," I said. I did not feel like arguing about a fish bowl. "Now, what would you recommend for cleaners for my house? I think I need glass and aluminum—"

"Sssss . . . sssss."

Pause.

"Sssssss . . . sssssssssss."

"Rattlesnake, what's wrong?" I asked, to no reply. Despite its early hour, the day had already been long, and Rattlesnake's shenanigans were stretching the hours and minutes even farther. He had already thrown himself into an argument with Goldfish (saltwater versus fresh) and eaten Mouse's sliver of Gruyère.

"You're going to need this cleaner for the roof . . . ," Mr. Hamilton said and looked at me oddly.

"Sssss . . . ssss . . . ssss."

"Rattlesnake, play with Tarantula." I held up a metal gallon of defogger. "Okay, now how exactly do I apply this?" I intended to make a quick exit from Das Haus Retro. Das store was starting to make me nervous.

"Sssssssssss."

"Behave yourself! Where is . . . ?"

Rattlesnake's playdate was nowhere to be found, however. I looked in my purse, a jumble of keys, coins, and insect rattles. I glanced at the luminous cement floor. Studying the window display—all things relating to the shag carpet—I finally looked up at Mr. Hamilton, who was already exasperated.

"You may want to check down the fifties aisle," Hamilton said with a subtle toss of the head.

I nodded quickly and looked to the flashing, lighted aisle signs. I made a beeline to eight.

I saw Tarantula first. He was resting on a blue satiny shirt. A shirt so expensive that it probably cost money just to look at. Tarantula looked comfortable, as if this blue perfectly pressed shirt were a place he could call home.

"Tarantula, stop climbing over that gentleman," I said. Awkwardly, I stopped just shy of the shirt. "Sir, I am so sorry. He won't hurt you. He's just playful," I apologized, and my eyes moved from the man's shirt to his face for the first time.

Each year, *Scientific Creatures* devoted its entire February issue to the human—typically my least favorite issue, as I have always found the species overrated. Often I jettisoned this installment without even creasing its spine. Once, I even wrote demanding a single copy refund.

But one year, *Scientific Creatures* and its team of researchers conducted a worldwide poll to discover what humans perceived as beautiful. The results were shocking. Apparently average features—familiar, in a sense—drive people wild. Individual average pieces fit together to form the puzzles that were Ingrid Bergman, Katharine Hepburn, John Wayne. We common folk were the exotic ones—lengthy limbs, pointy noses, bright red hair all coming together to make an ugly anomaly.

I suspected that *Scientific Creatures* would consider this man the perfect mean.

"I know. The tarantula is an amazing creature," he said, as he studied him. "And you, you are particularly beautiful."

He was referring to Tarantula, not me, of this I was convinced. I clumsily scooped Tarantula off of him, blushing as I brushed his shirt. He smiled crookedly.

XII

My creatures were trying to fall asleep, but I could not stop cleaning. I generally hated the task; tonight, however, was different. Lizard begged me to stop scrubbing the ceiling. Honeybee needed her beauty rest—her stripes faded slightly if she had less than twelve hours of sleep—and Bat could not go about his night business with the lights on. But I was focused on mold remover, window cleaner, defrost, defog, desmog, and him. Perhaps he thought *I* was beautiful, not Tarantula? The goldfish pond was deplorable; where did all this algae come from? Where did he live? Someplace fancy, obviously, if he was in Das Haus Retro. Millipede had to wipe his feet from now on; there were footprints, in sets of exactly one thousand, all over the floor. Where did all this dust come from? Termite will sweep it up tomorrow. No, I will clean it up now. And so the night went.

The next morning arrived quietly. Drops of dew on the glass roof altered the sun's hue. Determined to sweep away memories of this strange encounter with the rest of my life's debris, I made my cot and ventured into the main room.

The early dawn, when all of my creatures slept, was traditionally my favorite hour of the day. But at 7:05, I began to jar them awake.

"Termite," I said in his little ear, "time to wake up."

As was his custom, Termite jumped to his pinhead feet immediately, brushing sleep from his eyes.

I moved to Ladybug.

"Sweetheart," I said as I caressed her shell, "rise and shine. I'm going to make you a little breakfast."

Ladybug contorted one of her spindly black legs, attempting to touch her back. She struggled to reach her spotless, red shell.

Next was Tarantula. His long, furry tentacles clung to me as I proceeded to Jellyfish, Rat, Eel, Tortoise, Parrot, Flounder, Catfish, Sloth.

"Tarantula, climb up and wake Robin, please." Tarantula started up the bark conspiratorially. "Without disturbing Bat and Owl!" I said, but my order was too late. Tarantula had climbed over my night creatures. My day creatures giggled, and my air creatures began to play tag.

Four minutes later, all of my creatures were awake; ten minutes later, they had eaten breakfast. I retreated to my bedroom. The dew had melted away and I was again thinking of him.

Sleeplessness bled. Five days had passed and I was irritable.

My shift at the cacti park was crawling. I found myself staring at the invisible numbers on my watch wishing them to rearrange. . . . Six before one, seven before two. This desire was so keen that I caught myself musing the merits of moving my watch upside down and to the opposite wrist, in the hope time would follow its lead. Despite a thermometer's reality check, my forehead felt warm and my body ached.

In strict adherence to my new cleaning fetish, I decided to occupy myself with tidying the park, an almost insurmountable task. I was reshuffling the cacti: uprooting, depotting, deplanting, replanting, replacing. *M. bocasana* goes before *M. zeilmanniana* goes after *M. elongata* goes before *M. geminispina* goes after . . . daffodil?

"Dr. Cossman," I yelled across the Cactusarium, "why do we have a daffodil in here?"

"If you insist on rearranging the Cactusarium, please make sure to keep daffodil next to *M. rutilans*. I am attempting a little research project that demands their mutual affections." Cossman laughed maniacally.

The Dictator shifted his focus to Sylvia, a Cossman hanger-on who used the cacti park as a haven to smoke pot. Sylvia's off-the-shelf personality matched her plain looks. Even in my limited experience with creatures of the human kind, I could see that those were the girls who always found themselves in the most trouble.

"Excuse me, Dr. Cossman, but I think such a project could be dangerous to *M. rutilans*. It could kill him," I replied with force.

"Are you talking back to Dr. Cossman?" Sylvia bellowed.

"No, it's just . . ."

"I've had about enough out of you today," said Cossman. "And if you ever use that tone with me again, you'll be fired immediately. *M. rutilans* is a plant. We can always get another one. I don't know what's going on in that twisted little head of yours sometimes." Cossman glared maliciously, and he and Sylvia stole away to the janitor's closet.

M. rutilans looked at me with a tinge of appreciation.

"Don't worry, M., I'm not going to let that horrible man touch you." I touched his thorns, lightly. "You are . . ."

"Um, uh, sorry to interrupt."

I did not know how long he had been standing there. I hoped that he had not heard the argument with Cossman or the conversation I was having with *M. rutilans,* but I was not optimistic. I blushed, fingered my unbrushed hair, chewed on my necklace, and gawkily swayed from hip to hip—committing all four of my worst idiosyncrasies in the span of fifteen milliseconds, while he stood watching. I turned an even deeper shade of rouge as I began to speak.

"Um, no, you're not interrupting. I was just . . . ," I replied, chewing on my fake pearls as if they were gumballs. "Can I help you with something?"

"I don't know if you remember, but I met you at Das Haus Retro . . . ," he said. He was avoiding my eyes so intently that I wondered if he was talking to the flowering *Liliacaeae* next to me.

". . . ah, on Saturday, I guess it was." He fidgeted. If he weren't so suave, so debonair, I would have said he was nervous. But then I figured it must have been cool to fidget. So I fidgeted, too.

"I remember."

"You do?" he said, and, "Um, I'm Richard."

Now I was focused on the budding purple *Liliacaeae,* as if she had suddenly invented the lightbulb.

"Uh, it's nice to meet you," he said. "I hope you don't mind that I came by. I was just hoping we could continue our conversation about tarantulas. More. Again. Further. I enjoyed it."

"Yes. Me, too. I mean, I would love to," I declared, as I looked at him—I mean Richard. He looked at me back. It was a travesty anyone else could check "blue" under "eye color" on a driver's license form.

"Great."

"Great."

A long pause rested in the air. I rescued it just before it could fall asleep.

"Should I start?" I asked.

"Sure," he said, unsure.

"Well, I first got Tarantula when he was three months. I found him. Actually, *I* would be a misnomer. Grass Snake found him when we were out on a walk one day. . . ."

"Grass Snake?"

"Yes, that's a whole other story. . . ."

And so it began.

XIII

Although I had never come close to having a boyfriend before, I found myself self-importantly delving into the mind-set of the potential "boyfriend." My clairvoyant rationale dictated the following: The first day he did not call lest he appear overeager; the second because it was a Sunday, the Lord's Day, and it would be inappropriate; the third—well, that's where things sort of fell apart. I rewound and fast-forwarded our date in my mind and consulted with my creatures. They, too, were baffled and thought my rationale actually fell apart at Sunday, as this was no longer deemed a day of complete rest and no phone calls. Secretly, I think my creatures were relieved. They never had been good at sharing. The Monday after he didn't call I excused myself to bed early, pleading a slight ear infection.

As I lay in bed, I did have an ear infection. My right ear hummed a refrain that sang only one word: Richard. I was frustrated; I could not comprehend the grip this man had over me, nor could I begin to grasp its origins. Never had another person distracted me so, and I implored this source of wayward emotion to cease immediately. I did not know what it was about Richard that was ruining my sleep, disturbing my work in the cacti park, throwing my routine into anarchy. To be sure, Richard was beautiful, but his was not the in-your-face beauty of movie stars that caused housewives to put down their brooms and escape to a matinee. Richard's beauty was not even that of the quarterback of our high school football team, a boy whose All-American face, brute athleticism, and bad-boy cocaine addiction drove women wild. Richard's stone-chiseled face, his clear ennunciation, the unique hue of his fingernails, the way he licked his upper lip after he asked a question, the way he asked so many of them, the beautiful sound of grass when he brushed it with his black shoes: All of these were certainly appealing but, even in combination, should not have been making me ill with want. My emotional abacus was failing me, and I was an alien in my own body. Although it had admittedly thrown me into boredom and complaint, I now desperately wanted back the simple little life I had been living for the past nineteen years.

Das Haus Retro whistled and I came like a trained circus animal. Hamilton called on Wednesday to inform me that my preferred aluminum cleaner was marked ten percent off for seasonal housecleaning. The call and the sale were both out of character for Hamilton—he would not have wanted riffraff like me in his store even on the best of days, let alone those of clearance. But I pounced on the slight opening. The sale hours were 2 to 5 P.M. on Thursday and for preferred customers only. He hoped to see me there.

Much to my creatures' chagrin, I visited Das Haus Retro alone. Tarantula was particularly upset, as he took sole responsibility for drawing Richard and me together and had been repining for that blue satiny shirt since their first meeting. I was firm, however; and I left in my nicest pair of blue jeans and most flattering sweater, impervious to their complaining. I knew I was yearning for an improbable scenario, but I rolled the dice anyway.

"Thank you so much for coming."

"Thank you, Mr. Hamilton. Never a better time to stock up on aluminum cleaner," I said.

"And fastidious customers like you only shop for the best."

Why this newfound respect for me and my choice in cleaners?

"How's your glass house?" Hamilton continued.

"Fine, thank you," I replied. There was a big difference between a glass house and a glass greenhouse, but there was always later for that explanation.

"If you'll excuse me, I think I need something in aisle eight," I continued. "I'll be right back for the cleaner."

If my last brush with the Das Haus '50s aisle had been brief, this encounter could have filled a Modernism history requirement at a top-tier university. I spent little under an hour thumbing through cleaning supplies, furniture, and all forms of kitsch relating to the '50s home. I looked at my watch: 4:46. Then I heard: "Hi, Richard. Great to see you. How's the Yorff project coming?"

I had spent the past hour perusing '50s chaises in anticipation of Richard's attendance at the aluminum cleaner clearance sale. My first reaction to hearing the live rendition of his name: hide.

"I don't even want to talk about it. He asks for my creative input, but then ignores the advice in favor of something he's read in a magazine."

But where? Unless I was to scale the shelves, there was no place to hide in aisle eight. Besides, Hamilton would inevitably look for me at closing time when he noticed my bottle of Xall Xoff Aluminum Cleaner at the register. Perhaps I could escape to the '40s aisle.

"I'm sorry to hear that. Fortunately aficionados—moguls, if you will—such as yourself can afford to be selective with clients. Have you considered passing the project to one of your lesser competitors?" Hamilton asked.

Aficionado? Mogul? Lesser competitors? Yorff—wasn't he a movie star? No wonder he didn't call. Not only was this man out of my league, we weren't even playing the same sport. I made a split second decision: I was going to leave this with dignity.

Once in aisle nine, I breathed more deeply and reflected on the events of the last two minutes. I had been delusional. I had thrown my heart out there to someone who was probably juggling a number of them this very moment. I was sure he didn't even remember the damaged, wilted, and bruised one that was mine. He had probably had his assistant throw it in the Dumpster behind Yorff's house with the rest of the trash. He was now focused on the other hearts that belonged to girls who were beautiful and erudite and witty and . . .

"Hey. What a great surprise. It's good to see you."

Turn red. Put hand through hair. Grab necklace (which wasn't there). Sway.

"Hi. What are you doing in the forties aisle? I mean, how are you?" I replied.

"Oh, I'm just doing a walis nef house and need to find a kind of great doorstop for the fourth bedroom. . . ."

Walis what?

". . . God, I'm boring you. How are you?"

"Fine. I mean, compared to you, boring. What do you do? I mean, for a living?" I could not stop asking questions because I wanted to know more, much more.

"I don't know. It's so unimportant. I hate talking about work."

Relief. My talking about his work was like standing in bad lighting. Every wrinkle and flaw showed.

"It's really great to see you," he continued.

"You look amazing," I said. I had pulled my heart out of Yorff's trash and given it back to him. Please, sir, have your assistant throw it out again.

"No, I'm not . . ." He stopped and he pulled me apart with his eyes. "You're so pretty."

I wanted to press pause. No one had ever told me that before, let alone a man like Richard. I needed a moment to regain my footing. He obliged.

After a few seconds he continued, with a touch of fluster, "Would you be interested in going to the thirties aisle with me?"

We went to the '30s aisle and beyond that afternoon, peppering each other with questions. I felt as if I were on a game show with no wrong answers but a huge jackpot to be paid out in coins of platinum. Richard told me he was thirty-eight, an earth sign, and made his living designing people's houses. He seemed oddly ashamed of his occupation. In fact, in the split second it took me to formulate a question about his glamorous job, Richard had already leapfrogged the subject of work, instead focusing on his wobbly childhood and adolescence. He explained that he had run away from his Southern family when he was still a boy. In response to my startled facial expression, he quickly added that he had left his parents who, in the simplest terms, had never loved him. I did not believe this, as such a mistake seemed impossible.

I chronicled my life; first Daddy and his premature departure, then Mama and hers. I squirmed a lot while admitting to my troubled past and words kept getting stuck on the roof of my mouth, but Richard only prodded me further with his endless eyes. I found myself surprised when I confessed to Richard my childhood dream of becom-

ing a veterinarian and admitted that, in my mind, a candle of jealousy
still burned for Kris Tina Woo, my teenage friend gone brilliant architect. Although I preached contentedness at the cacti park, I did so in a
way that said, "I hate the place," and he read the cue perfectly. When
he asked me what I wanted to do with my life now, I reverted to the
safety subject of my greenhouse. Richard casually revealed that he
had once lived in a glass house, too. It was a noytra, he said, that a lover
had bought him for a present.

That statement had claws. It clung to me desperately through the
early evening when we parted ways. I could not shake the thought
even when I climbed into bed, covered in starlight and giddy with
nerves. Each time I closed my eyes, I thought of Richard lying in a
glass house with his lover. I could see his sharp profile as he gazed at
her; his isoscelean nose, his chiseled cheekbones, that blue vein which
protruded from the side of his head and screamed *man*.

Little droplets of sweat were glued to the diminutive pieces of dry
skin on my scalp and the arches of my eyebrows. I did not want to
close my eyes again, for fear that the image of Richard and his lover
would continue to haunt me as a record that skipped on its weakest
track.

"Tarantula, honey, come here and talk to me for a moment," I said.
The only reply was the wind swirling around the exteriors of the
greenhouse.

"Daddy Long Legs, sweet pea, would you like to lie down with
me? You can even share my pillow." Daddy Long Legs loved to sprawl
out, octopus-like, on a fluffy white pillow.

"I prefer to fall asleep on a cold cement floor rather than share a
warm pillow with a woman of a cold heart," he declared.

"Nightingale," I began. "Come closer so I can tell you a story of
love and murder and revenge, set in Ancient Rome with witches and

fairies." Nightingale loved nothing more than an epic love story, yet tonight he feigned sleep and read to himself in his mind, proving a point which had already been proven twice over.

I continued this ritual with each one of my 310 creatures. All pretended to be asleep, yet 620 pairs of eyes glistened in the darkness. Jealousy pumped through their little veins like lava, and suspicion settled in their creaky bones. They were gluttons, these heartless, gutless creatures, and I did not understand why I loved them so much. But I did.

XIV

Richard disappeared. It was as if he had wrapped up my smiles and put them in a large bag, toting them to his mysterious destination where they would remain until our next meeting, if there were to be one. I could not take solace in my creatures; since I had met Richard, they had been surly, almost feral. Many had come down with mild cases of the flu, others were petulant and refractory. Some even tried to escape the Case Study House. One particularly stormy evening, I awoke to find my beloved creatures making a sixteen-foot-high creature ladder, with Sparrow, its pinnacle, reaching just short of the ceiling latch.

Tonight my creatures were frolicsome. Despite the late hour, they were not succumbing toward the world of Zs; they were defiantly turning to the world of As—the world of being awake.

"Will you please be quiet?" I asked, but the words echoed off the glass house's walls and sunk into the cement floor.

I retreated to my bedroom, turned off the glowing bulb, settled into my cot. The constellations were out full force this evening; I could see the Big Dipper, the North Star, Orion.

I closed my eyes, but chuckles, giggles, and conspiratorial guffaws floated in from the main room. I had a sense my creatures were getting into trouble. I groggily left my bedroom and ventured into the main living area.

My creatures were playing with a crumpled piece of paper.

"Please," I yelled. "Get to sleep *now*."

I walked over and grabbed the paper, furious at them for their antics, for ruining my sleep, for taking something that belonged to me. I had never reprimanded my creatures in such a forceful way before.

I returned to my room and smoothed out the piece of paper. On it, written in perfect penmanship, was: I will be there Tuesday at twenty-one o'clock.

I put my creatures to bed early on Tuesday and instructed even my night creatures to remain in the greenhouse in silence. The flutter of wings, the cool splash of a late night swim, the surface bubbling of breath in the pond, even the tiptoe of multiple insect feet on the cement floor: None of these were acceptable distractions. Perhaps this intolerability was unfair, an unnecessary restriction. But I only thought of Richard now.

I wore a long pastel dress that had belonged to Mama. It was a nightgown, really, but no one would have known; its complex print in woven silk hid those distinguishing characteristics that a nightgown is supposed to flaunt. I began to wait for Richard an hour before nine (in case he was early) and stood at the end of the dirt driveway. I hoped the gesture would not make me appear overeager. I strongly suspected, however, that that was just the thing dating books and feminists would have advised against.

Not a single car passed between the hours of eight o'clock and nine o'clock. When the grating of rubber tires on the rough road penetrated the air, it was like the air had been waiting for this sound for a very long time and had gone completely quiet on its arrival. I could not have imagined waiting one minute longer for him; my heart would have burst.

Richard drove a fancy truck; it was black.

"Hey," he said as he pulled to the side of the road. He opened his window (the automatic kind) before he stopped the truck, and I wondered if he was excited to see me, too.

Richard stepped out of his car. His black shoes rubbed the dirt and made a magnificent crumbling noise.

"It's great to see you," he said. This standard greeting managed to sound brand new. My hips swayed so exaggeratedly that I thought they might disconnect from their joints.

Richard looked down at his outfit, his pinstripe shirt and baggy blue jeans.

"I should go home and change. Your dress . . . You look beautiful," Richard said.

He hadn't noticed I was wearing a nightgown.

"No. You do," I said quickly. I looked down and crinkled the nightgown's silk in my fingers, hoping it could absorb my nervousness. "You always do."

Richard flushed a bit, as if he had just spent an afternoon in the sun. He looked to the Case Study House. "Your house is kind of brilliant. Who was the architect?"

"I can't remember," I finally said. "A junior architect or something, I think. I mean, it must be someone who really doesn't know what she, I mean, *he's* doing because everything's always breaking."

"Oh," Richard said, and he refocused on me. Intently, with those blue blue eyes and that crooked crooked smile. "I just want to know everything about you. That's why I asked."

Richard opened the heavy passenger door and helped me into his truck.

"What is your favorite fruit?" Richard asked.

"Hmmm . . . Can I think about it?" I asked. I sat beside Richard in his truck. The dashboard glowed blue lights.

"If you think very quickly," Richard began. "Your response is going to determine which exit we take. See, we just passed Cherry."

I turned around on cue and, sure enough, we had just passed a sign that read "Exit 34—Cherry." A sign in front of us said "Pineapple Next Exit."

"This is too much pressure. Can you decide?" I was worried I would choose a fruit Richard did not like. I wanted him to be happy.

"Can *I* decide what *your* favorite fruit is? It doesn't work like that, Zor."

Zor.

"Are there any fruits you positively don't like?" This question was important.

Richard slowed down a bit, leaned over, and his lips were so close they almost swept my cheek. "Well, I got really hurt in Grapefruit once."

My eyes widened. Thoughts of Richard's past were generally unwelcome; I would sometimes even try to make myself believe that he was born the moment we met. "What happened?" I asked, although there was a part of me that did not want to hear the response.

"I jumped up to pick a grapefruit from a tree and a thorn scratched my forehead," he said self-consciously. "I still have a scar."

I looked at Richard's forehead. It was flawless.

"Well, we shouldn't go to Grapefruit then. Bad memories."

"If you like grapefruits . . . ," Richard began earnestly, in appeasement.

"No, no," I interrupted. I looked away from Richard, at the exit sign for Pineapple looming near.

"Let's go to Pineapple," I said.

"Are you choosing Pineapple because it's the next exit, or because it's your favorite fruit?"

"Um, because it's the next exit," I responded with a smile. "Apples are my favorite fruit."

Richard placed his fingers gently on my hair. They just rested there, afraid to get tangled up in a mess which they couldn't get out of.

"Red or Green?"

"Green, please."

"Green Apple, it is."

The Orchards of Green Apple could have supplied the entire universe with their fruit. Trees sat in long rows on perfectly sheared, bright green grass. The trees' plump apples were ripe and emitted a candied fragrance; the size of each would have been enough for an entire pie. I could not help but think that even nature—even apples and blades of grass and trees—was in best form for Richard. Nature wanted his attention.

Violin music sang for Richard and me as we sipped glasses of green apple juice and ate snacks. "This is my favorite symphony," I said, as I fed crumbs to nearby squirrels.

"You know this?" Richard asked in amazement.

"It's Chopin's 'Fantaisie in A major.' It was the first full symphony I learned on the violin," I answered, though not boastfully.

"You play the violin?" Richard asked. "I have absolutely no musical talent. My whole life I've wanted to learn an instrument, but never had the time or the skill."

"Oh, well, I learned the violin when I was young, and I think that helps. As a matter of fact, someone once told me that it's very difficult to learn the violin after your twelfth birthday. I could teach you, though."

"I'd be too embarrassed," Richard said and looked down at his cracker. I furrowed my eyebrows and scolded myself. Why did I have to discuss the only thing in the world I was good at? I was becoming like Kris Tina, like Zoë.

"How did you decide to become a designer?" I asked quickly.

"I don't know. It just sort of happened," Richard said deliberately. He stole a long sip of his apple juice, and I could almost see it drizzle down the inside of his throat. "Green apples are my favorite fruit, too," he said.

"I'm really glad I picked it then. No pun intended," I said and we both smiled. "Did you want to become a designer even when you were a little boy?" I asked.

"I really wanted to be an architect," Richard began. "I remember when I was young, maybe twelve, I hocked my guitar for a video camera. I used to walk around the neighborhood and videotape houses. My friends thought I was crazy. They were skateboarding and making out with girls, and I was videotaping tract homes. I called the tape 'Home Movie.' I thought I was so clever." Richard's smile was nostalgic.

"And then what happened?"

"And then I grew up . . ." He faded out. "I guess it just slipped away."

I looked at him lovingly, as if perhaps my eyes would make up for his lost dream. I knew they would not though.

"You could probably still be an architect," I said. I looked down at the plaid blanket as I said this, afraid I was saying the wrong thing. "I mean, if you really wanted to."

Richard looked at me closely and he smiled.

"I guess I don't really want to anymore."

"Why?" I asked.

"Well, I think I probably wouldn't be any good at it." He added quickly, "I hate talking about me. It's so uninteresting."

Usually it was now that he would ask a question to change the subject. Tonight, though, he didn't. Instead he eventually continued.

"My life is full of things left unfinished."

"What kind of things?" I asked.

A worm wiggled out from the core of Richard's green apple. Richard didn't notice, though, and the worm crawled onto the blanket.

"I don't know. Places, I guess. Perhaps, well, perhaps even people."

"People?" I paused. "You mean, a relationship?"

The violin music was off-tune. The apples had turned sour.

"I'm boring you."

"Why don't you finish them?" I asked, at once realizing his self-deprecation could be manipulative.

"I'm not making any sense. I'm just talking in circles."

It was quiet and I felt as if the air was an enemy. I looked at Richard's forehead again and traced its crevices. He was not going to respond.

"Where is your grapefruit scar?" I finally asked in a whisper, and Richard silently moved my left thumb to his upper forehead. Richard was silent and he continued to lead my thumb with his.

"I want you to be a veterinarian, Zor," Richard finally said with feeling.

"But, I can't . . ."

"I can't, but you can."

And for the remainder of the time at the Orchards of Green Apple, I did not think about veterinary school at all. I thought of something much more important, much more current. I thought about how I could stop myself from falling in love with the mysterious man who sat next to me.

K ris Tina Woo peppered me with incessant postcard re-
minders that she was on an exotic journey, but I was not
jealous. It was an odd feeling; I had spent my younger
years looking at Zoë and Kris Tina from afar and close-up, wanting
desperately to be inserted into their glamorous lives. Yet, now, I
wanted only my own.

Kris Tina's first postcard had arrived from Beijing, China, and featured a photograph of Dorsey Monument Two. It was an Asian-
looking skyscraper with exotic lines and ancient characters, a
skyscraper so important that people even had to purchase tickets to
see it. Kris Tina's short summary was full of her lofty prose—*I did not
think it possible, but Dorsey Monument Two is more breathtaking in real life
than in my textbook. Floor seventeen features incredible lines; I cannot help
but make the obvious comparison to the residence I have designed*—and I was
grateful I was able to read, not have to hear, the young architect's
haughtiness. The second postcard, from the "perpetually war-torn
country of Iran," featured a picture of Architect Dorsey's impressive
War Memorial. Both postcards featured the identical addendum in

her architect's print—*Are you taking copious notes on Woo Case Study House #1's superior livability?*

The third postcard was postmarked in Cape Town and marked urgent. Kris Tina indicated that a terrible thing had happened; someone had stolen *Dorsey: The Unfinished Works* from her South African hotel. She was in inconsolable despair, and needed me immediately to visit Das Haus Retro. Mr. Hamilton had one copy of the text; I could Xerox it, Kris Tina asserted, and send it to Cape Town where she would await its arrival. She ended the note, "Today is not soon enough!"

And, indeed, today was not soon enough. One hundred thirteen hours had passed since Richard and I had been at the orchard, yet once again, he had not called. Despite the fact that I had determined to become more aggressive in my tactics, days without Richard were exactly that: days without Richard. I had no address for him, no contact information, not even a last name. I knew pieces of his unhappy childhood, I heard vague particulars on his daily events. I would occasionally prod enough to receive a nibble of personal preferences—Orion over the Little Dipper, for example—but even these generally eluded me.

Richard never mentioned a single client, he never spoke of friends or even a residence. My sole human connection to Richard was Mr. Hamilton. This was unfortunate, as Mr. Hamilton's icy veneer and lofty design taste were severe barriers. Until Kris Tina's desperate postcard, there was little reason for me to visit Das Haus Retro.

Now I drove to the storefront. Only one car was parked there. It was not a black truck.

Das Haus Retro was silent when I entered. No customers flitted about, Mr. Hamilton did not greet me in the foyer. I looked around. I had spent time in the '30s aisle with Richard; I had first met him in the '50s aisle; I had hidden from him in the '40s aisle. Aisle one featured animal enclosures; I was aware of this from my experience with Flounder's carrying bowl. Where, I wondered, was the book aisle?

"May I help you?" Hamilton was tense, but he no longer looked at me with condescension.

"Hello, Mr. Hamilton."

He looked at me curiously. I liked this. Besides Richard, no one looked at me with interest.

I pulled Kris Tina's postcard from my purse. I presented it to Hamilton.

"I received this today. Apparently someone has brazenly stolen Kris Tina's architecture textbook." I said this with a bit of sarcasm, but Mr. Hamilton did not laugh.

Instead, the man read the postcard twice or three times, his eyes skating along its surface as if it were fragile ice. He nodded as he read it, but not to me. The front of the card featured a picture of Dorsey Monument Four.

"He was very talented, you know."

Mr. Hamilton looked at me closely when he said this, as if soliciting my opinion. I looked down at my tattered clothing, my straggly hair, my gangly legs. I knew nothing of architecture or Architect Dorsey, and Hamilton must have known this.

I nodded.

"He could have been the premier architect." Mr. Hamilton emphasized the word *the*. "He was, for a brief time. Before it all fell apart."

"Do you know what happened? To Architect Dorsey, I mean?"

Mr. Hamilton looked at me for a long moment.

"Would you like to follow me?"

"Of course." I suddenly missed my creatures. I wished I had brought Tarantula.

Mr. Hamilton led me to the back of the store and stopped at a glass case. It was locked, and he pulled out a long and rusty key.

There, behind glass, rested *Dorsey: The Unfinished Works*. Unlike Kris Tina's copy, this one was pristine. No scratches, no curled pages, no cracked binding. It was as if the text had never been read.

"I believe this is what Kris Tina Woo is seeking," Mr. Hamilton said, as he gazed at the book.

I smiled. "Yes, that's the text. She used to carry it on the school bus." I realized how little I knew Kris Tina anymore. Perhaps I had never really known her. "How many copies are there? A long time ago, Kris Tina had mentioned it was out of print."

Mr. Hamilton smiled a sad smile and looked at the textbook in its glass case.

"Only three." He paused. "One in Cape Town, one here in Das Haus Retro . . ." He faded out.

"No wonder she's so possessive of it. I had no idea. Where is the third?" I asked.

Hamilton was quiet, and I was afraid to turn around lest the aisles disappear. Overcome with unease, I at once felt as if I was discovering too much. But, too much what?

"Only one person knows. Perhaps you should ask him."

"Who?" I asked. "Who knows where the third copy is?"

I looked at Mr. Hamilton with questioning eyes, but his were transparent. He did not respond.

"Who is it that knows?"

"Richard Dorsey," he said, and suddenly it all made sense.

I only wanted to look at the textbook, but Mr. Hamilton kept it locked behind the glass and insisted that he personally send a copy to

Kris Tina. I returned home empty-handed. My creatures were again wild, playing, arguing. They were oblivious, of course, to the irreversible change that had occurred in my life that afternoon at Das Haus Retro. Suddenly, I felt angry at them for their ignorance.

I settled in my room and laid on my cot.

Richard, Richard Dorsey. Richard, Richard Dorsey. I repeated this aloud many times, hoping it would eventually feel normal. It didn't, though. Richard Dorsey was famous and beautiful and intriguing and smart; what would he see in a plain girl like me? I stared at Kris Tina's postcards again—Dorsey Monument Two, Dorsey Monument Three, Dorsey Monument Four—and I tried to learn more about him through his designs, through the grainy photographs. He had traveled, his monuments reached to the sky. What did this say about him? Kris Tina and *Dorsey: The Unfinished Works* had alluded to a mysterious residence; where was the residence and for whom had it been designed? Had it been for a woman? Had she been the reason Richard Dorsey's life had fallen apart? Or had the reason been intellectual? I thought back to Zoë Christie and that day at her architectural estate many years ago. Even then, Richard Dorsey had repeatedly disappeared, but to where? Did Mr. Hamilton know? I replayed that day at the Christies' architectural estate in my mind again. "Zorka, never fall in love with a ghost," Mrs. Christie had said, staring at diamonds in the crowded sky.

XVI

Preparations for the Annual Firefly Dinner Dance were underway and I had been kicked off the Steering Committee. The vote was unanimous (twelve in favor, zero against) and the wording strong ("She shall have no part in planning or execution of such aforementioned event"). The entire committee—Salmon, Cicada, Eel, Songbird, Cricket, Scorpion, Turtle, Seahorse, Crane, Tapeworm, Locust, and the Chairwoman Firefly herself—opposed my involvement with the gala event and froze me out of the planning process. The sentiments of the Committee were reflective of those of the entire group. On my return home from the cacti park, a hush would fall over my creatures, as if I were a great enemy trying to foil their plans or take hostage their nationals. Even Termite, once my only friend, turned his back on me when I asked him to assist in a routine household chore.

While my creatures spent their spare hours devising further ways to snub and punish me for my incessant thoughts of Richard Dorsey, the source of this vexation was still missing. I had fallen in love 310 times previously, and I had always found the objects of my devotion to be accessible, simple folk who longed for a few extra nibbles of pretzels and a handful of kind words a day. Richard's prolonged disappearance was throwing me into frenzy.

My creatures scattered in my wake as I moved across the Case Study House. I looked through the house's transparent walls; perhaps the outside would calm my mind. My creatures watched while I sat on the grass and looked up at the sun.

There was no reason for him to like me, really. Richard Dorsey had rejected Zoë Christie. I thought of Zoë's Modernist locker, the erotic orchid Richard had given her, the streamlined mirror. Zoë wore colored eye shadow, she lived on an architectural equestrian estate, she was the jockey of a future champion thoroughbred. I did not even know how to apply eye shadow, I lived in a glass greenhouse, my creatures were certainly not champion animals.

My creatures exchanged bewildered glances as they looked at me. My mind whirled. Perhaps the answer to Richard's disappearances was close by. I just had to get in the car and drive there.

The Ix Public Library had been through many transformations in its fourteen-year life. Inaugurated as an extension of the elderly care center down the street, the public library had first been a safe haven for senior citizens. But a fire ravaged the Ix Public Library one evening, and the library's impressive planning board forgot to plan for wheelchair accessibility. It was thus that Governor Gary Jones suggested the library would be the ideal place for local criminals to toil for their community service hours. This mandate turned on the governor when an entire third-grade Richard Scarry reading group become addicted to LSD. In the investigation, all roads led back to the deputy chief librarian, whose priors included killing his ex-girlfriend in cold blood with a knife.

Never to be swayed by grammar school drug addiction, the new Governor Bob Smith boldly proclaimed the Ix Public Library a bastion for child geniuses. Those unique specimens would be ideal librarians, he said. Never mind child labor laws or the fact that four-year-olds could not reach the high shelves. The library was now staffed by a handful of preteen aspiring recluses.

Unfortunately for me, this library was the only institution in a one-hundred-mile radius that housed the key to Richard Dorsey's heart: *The World Book Encyclopedia*. I took a deep breath as I approached the library, hoping that I would find a gray-haired woman with owl-like glasses and an old-fashioned rubber stamp waiting. . . .

"Hello, may I be of assistance?" The five-year-old wore Coke-bottle glasses, a striped tie, and toted a book entitled *Physics and Aristotle: The Untold Inverse Relationship*.

"Hi," I said to the top of the child's blond bowl cut. "I won't take up much of your time."

"Time. What is time anyway? According to Nietzsche . . ."

"Yes," I interrupted. "All I really need is access to *The World Book Encyclopedia*. I'm doing a bit of research."

Child Genius led me to the reference section. "As you may be aware, *The World Book Encyclopedia* generally gives a thirty-thousand-foot view of any topic. If we could head into Conference Room #2 and discuss your research goals more thoroughly, I may be able to point you to more specific reference tools." Child Genius pointed to a wall of books dedicated to Zimbabwean Watches. "I have memorized the texts of all subjects from Z to Q, so if your subject falls in those letters, you're in luck."

"Oh," I said. "Well, my boyfriend is a world famous, um, uh, architect or something like that, so I'm helping him with some research." Boyfriend. That word belonged in bright lights over Broadway, in blinking red letters outside a hospital.

"I see," he said stretching it out like taffy at the county fair. "In layman's terms, therefore, you would be seeking information on architecture."

"Yes, you could say that," I said. Had I ever behaved like this?

"Damn. This isn't your lucky day, ma'am." Child Genius emphasized the poor rhyme and adjusted his oversized frames. "I am very good with rhymes. I'm publishing my first book of poetry. Look for it on shelves later this year."

I nodded, and Child Genius did not skip an iambic beat. "I apologize profusely that I cannot be of assistance. I anticipate arriving at 'Architecture' mid-December. Perhaps I could interest you in finding information on turn-of-the-century teacups?"

"Maybe next time," I said, grateful this show-off would not be the one to guide me to the magnificent world of noytras. "I think I should be able to find the information I need in *The World Book,* but thank you for your sage advice."

"Sage, yes." Child Genius rubbed his nose. "Here is the Reference Section. Please do not hesitate to call me if I can be of further assistance." Child Genius jotted down the word 'sage' on a pink slip of paper. "My name is Chucky."

The boy disappeared, I suspected to research the meaning of 'sage.'

I opened *The World Book, Volume 14*—Nabakov to Ozone—and looked up that enigmatic word *noytra.* Alfred Noyes was a famous early twentieth-century poet. U Nu was a Burmese politician and statesman. But what was a noytra? I looked up *noitra.* Noise is a random or unwanted sound. Nok was a West African civilization that flourished from 500 B.C. to A.D. 200.

Perhaps a noytra, whatever that was, was not famous enough to catch the eye of *The World Book*. I decided to go on to *mees*. Richard tossed around this term even more often than *noytra*, so *The World Book* most likely tossed it around as well. Meerkat is a small burrowing animal of Africa. Megalithic Monuments are structures built of large stones by prehistoric people for burial or religious purposes. I tried every other imaginable spelling, *meis, meas,* to no avail. Ditto for *walis, lawtner, wecksler*.

"Chucky," I shouted. Tears were forming in my eyes now. Was Richard speaking a language I would never decipher?

Chucky arrived eating noodles from an oversized bowl. "You called?" he asked rhetorically. "I'm just eating some spaghetti with *sage*. Is something wrong?"

"I'll tell you what's wrong. Something's gravely wrong with your *World Book Encyclopedia*. I think there are pages missing."

"Impossible."

I opened up the encyclopedia. "As you can see . . . ," I began.

"No, I cannot see." Chucky inhaled a long spaghetti noodle and reached for *The World Book*. "You are usurping my view."

I tugged at the encyclopedia.

"I'm sorry to bruise your ego, but I don't think that was a proper use of usurp," I said with an unknown maliciousness.

"Give me this!" Chucky had resorted to age-appropriate behavior.

"I'm not finished with it yet," I yelled back.

The N encyclopedia was the rope in our tug-of-war. Chucky had tossed aside his sage-sprinkled spaghetti and his baby teeth were clenched in ferocity; I was pulling at an encyclopedia which . . .

Which what? Why had this N encyclopedia once seemed important?

I relinquished control of the encyclopedia and Chucky flew backward across the room, directly into the shelf of books relating to Peruvian Drug Cartels. The dusty hardbacks and their metal bookends buried Chucky and pinned him on the library floor. He screamed.

At once, docile library patrons hovered around Chucky and glared at me. I was the crazy one. Why had I driven twenty-one miles on this wild goose chase? Did I need to be fluent in Richard's language for him to understand me? If so, why couldn't I just ask *him* for some reference books? I was not going to be Mama. Richard Dorsey was not going to make me Mama.

I gathered my belongings while Chucky stood on wobbly feet and taped together the N volume of the encyclopedia, reconnecting Alfred Noyes and U Nu.

"Excuse me," Chucky began. "I need you to leave your address in case my supervisor needs to discuss with you the events of this afternoon or bill you for the invisible tape used in the repairs." He chuckled as I scribbled the address.

"Thanks again for all your help," I said, this time earnestly. I closed the door behind me.

It was pouring snails and dragonflies and butterflies. Windshield wipers were useless, my vision was cloudy, and I was counting the miles to home. I allowed my mind to wander wherever it pleased—to the open windows of the greenhouse, to the Firefly Dance, to Daddy Long Legs's persistent stomach ailment—just not to the events which had transpired at the Ix Public Library that afternoon or the man whose whims inadvertently caused said disaster. I ramped up the volume of the radio to try to drown out the white noise that was Richard Dorsey.

When I arrived home, the greenhouse was lit from the inside and a truck sat in its dirt driveway. My heart shuddered and my first thought was the safety of the creatures.

The second was Richard Dorsey. Radiant, he was surrounded by my creatures, a circle with a radius four deep. Tarantula hugged the clock around Richard's neck.

"Abyssal Dire Rat is my favorite. Do you know what his secret power is?" Richard asked his enraptured audience.

They cooed, their wings fluttered in anticipation.

"Well, and this I think is kind of genius, he turns his victims into their greatest enemies so they have to fight against themselves."

My creatures shouted in unison.

"Why does Absyssal Dire Rat do this, Mr. Richard?" asked Mosquito, the type who rarely spoke up in class and generally sat in the back row.

"Um. Let's see. It is the master's assumption that people are loath to turn into those whom they despise most. According to this tenet, we should all look at ourselves through the eyes of our worst enemy. Then and only then will we understand ourselves. Does this make sense to you all?"

Richard looked out on the sea of creatures.

"Now, before we go on to the next guy, can someone tell me where your mom is?"

I held my breath just waiting for one of my creatures to say, "She's at the library trying to find out what a noytra is." Richard would run for his life.

But Boa held up another Dungeons and Dragons trading card. Dungeons and Dragons was my creatures' favorite pastime, but I had not been aware Richard shared this passion. It seemed incongruous for a man of his stature. I smiled to myself as I stared through the glass. "Who is this, Mr. Richard?" Boa asked, politely.

"That is Troglodyte, Boa," Richard began, with the patience of a kindergarten teacher. "Do you know what a troglodyte is?"

This was a word I had yet to teach them in vocabulary class.

"No, what is a trogolotided?" Jellyfish often had trouble with pro-
nunciation.

Richard smiled. "That's a good question, Jellyfish. I don't know."

My creatures laughed and held Richard in even more esteem for
this goofy admission.

"A troglodyte is a person considered to be reclusive, reactionary, or
out of date," I said quietly.

Richard looked at me, and his smile was a simple pill that offered
instant relief from the past eight days.

"Use it in a sentence," Richard challenged, half facetiously, as he escorted me into the circle and awkwardly put his arm around my waist.

"I had always considered myself to be of average beauty and a
fashion troglodyte, yet for a reason which was just beyond my
grasp . . ." I paused here, and I whispered in Richard Dorsey's ear,
"You are here."

Richard kissed me on the cheek and then gave me a hug. His hugs
were surrounded by fireworks.

"Bravo!" my creatures shouted. If their cheers were for the return
of normalcy, their standing ovation was, to be certain, for Richard.
His spell could bring an entire kingdom of creatures to their feet,
while bringing me to my knees. Its reverse effects were astounding.

"It's good to see you," he mumbled too low for my creatures to hear.

"It's good to see you, too," I replied, and we both looked away.

In an attempt to focus on anything but the face I had waited days
to see, I looked at the greenhouse's glass. It was no longer pouring
snails and dragonflies and butterflies.

It was something else, but I could not put my finger on what that
something was.

XVII

Kris Tina Woo was now in Riyadh. Her postcard was perfunctory; she had received a copy of *Dorsey: The Unfinished Works* from Mr. Hamilton and had actually enjoyed the snag in her schedule. Cape Town was splendid, and her extended stay had permitted her to assist the local police in the theft investigation. Kris Tina departed South Africa with a snippet of information on Architect Dorsey as well: Sources said the architect had seemed distracted when designing the Cape Town monument. He had sent multiple telegrams from the local post, he had spent extended hours staring at the mountains. The recipients and content of the telegrams were unknown, however, and the architect's thoughts had been forever lost in the jaggedy-edged hills.

I stared intently at the picture of Dorsey Monument Five. I had long ago read that it was the most complex of the commissions. The Monument was the shape of an oil well (half of one, of course) and contained a conference room for royalty; chairs were thrones and coffeepots were made of rubies.

I looked at the postcard again, and *M. rutilans* leaned in. Again, my thoughts ran away. Although we had been spending most of our free hours together, Richard still had not revealed to me his last name or former occupation. I guess he believed that lost glory was sometimes worse than no glory at all.

"This, M., is Dorsey Monument Five. It's in Riyadh, which is very far away."

M. nodded. A few other cacti leaned in as well, interested in what I had to say. The Cactusarium was quiet.

"It's very impressive. My *friend*"—I put emphasis on this word—"designed it."

"Um, uh, do you have a friend who designs things?"

I turned around; there stood Richard with his off-center smile. In alarm, I dropped the postcard in the dirt. Richard leaned over to pick it up, but fortunately *M. rutilans* grabbed it first. The cactus placed it in my canvas bag. He then wrapped his long and spindly arms behind his back. I breathed a quick sigh of relief.

I looked at Richard again, and I instantly forgot my unease. All that he had designed, all that had transpired before the moment we met, none of it mattered because Richard Dorsey was here.

"You look beautiful," I said before I could stop myself. All of those perfect features on one person: It wasn't fair. I smiled, and Richard looked down.

"I don't understand why you say that. I feel like sometimes you're looking at someone, or something, behind me or something." Richard patted his cropped hair and looked at me again. "God, what a dumb sentence."

He blushed, and I looked at *M. rutilans* so he wouldn't notice I noticed.

"No, I'm sure you're sick of that specific compliment. You must hear it all the time," I said. Suddenly the metal watering can became very intriguing; I fingered it and averted my eyes from Richard's long stare.

"No." Richard turned quiet, as if in contemplation. "I, well, I'm just not used to people saying it about me. A long time ago, people used to say it about . . ." Richard tilled the dirt with his sandal. "It's stupid. I'm boring you."

"You never bore me. I want to learn more about you."

He was quiet now.

"My life." Richard paused; perhaps he felt his life was something very separate from the rest of him. "It somehow took a wrong turn somewhere. And now I'm here."

Sadness overwhelmed me. A wrong turn had led him to a wrong outcome.

"That came out wrong. I didn't mean that. Like it sounded." Richard looked down again, and he touched my arm. I should have been happy, since I wasn't used to human touch. But instead the gesture felt forced.

I poured a little water from the sprinkling can on my fingers. It felt cold.

"Zorka."

"What?"

"I want to take you somewhere."

Later we were on our way to somewhere. Although we had only driven a few miles, I was lost. Richard never failed to surprise me. In the past week we had been to a wax factory, a skeleton museum, a voodoo parlor. It was astounding all of these places existed just beyond the reach of my knowledge. I wondered if other people had spent dates molding movie stars out of wax. Perhaps they even pricked voodoo dolls of me with pins.

The lighthouse was not really a lighthouse at all. Sure, the externalities were there: The structure was tall, surrounded by a big pile of boulders, and emanated a bright, far-reaching strobe. If one could coin a reservoir owned by *Power and Electric* as a body of water, it was located on one; if one could call the chain-smoking Mr. Salz a keeper, it had one. But as we drove up, I could tell that this was not a lighthouse of the usual sort.

We approached it together. His pinstriped arm brushed my bare one; although it seemed like a mistake, there was a part of me that thought perhaps it was premeditated.

"Where are the ships?" I asked nervously. I was always worried I would say the wrong thing around him.

Richard smiled, as if my naïveté was special.

"This lighthouse doesn't guide ships," was his response, and it was knowing, certain, perhaps even a bit sad.

"Oh," I said, and again pinstriped cloth met bare arm. This time it was on purpose, I could tell.

The rocky, jagged boulders were our destination. Their speckles looked like diamonds and sparkled in the lighthouse's soft strobe, its sweeping support. Richard and I sat down on the rocks; despite their rough appearance, they were remarkably comfortable.

Richard tentatively placed his arm behind me.

"Have you been here before?" he asked quietly, almost in a whisper.

"No," I answered, "I didn't even know it was here." I leaned backward a little bit so I could feel Richard's arm. An arm behind me became an arm around me.

The reservoir water lapped the surface, washed over the boulders. I looked at Richard closely, and for the first time noticed a chain around his neck. It was thickly woven gold, and I reached for it, primarily as an excuse to touch the soft, hairless skin beneath.

The chain led to an antique gold watch.

"What is this?" I asked tentatively. Richard looked down at the rocks. They were exposed, submerged, depending on the tides of the reservoir.

"It's a clock," he finally answered.

"Do you wear it all the time?"

"Yes." His response was almost apologetic, as if the clock were in some way a sin.

I touched the skin below the clock. It felt different than any other skin I had ever felt.

"That feels nice."

I squiggled. I had the power to make someone feel nice. Had I been born with this power? Or was it recently acquired?

"Thank you," I said, and continued to focus on Richard's collarbone. His eyes were closed now, and I had my first glimpse of his eyelids. They looked fragile.

"This is a very special lighthouse," Richard began, his eyes still closed. "It's not a lighthouse for ships. It's a lighthouse for lost souls."

I traced shapes on Richard's chest now. A ladybug with a single black spot. A puffy storm cloud. A dense comet with a long tail.

"What do you mean?" I asked.

"Well, people come here when they . . ." Richard faded out.

"When they what?" I drew a heart with an arrow. "Are we lost? Is that why we're here?"

"Do you ever feel lost, Zorka?" Richard asked passionately.

I paused, looked very closely at Richard's convex chest. It looked like it was trying to escape the confines of his skin.

"Well, I did, I think. But not right now." I smiled. "Perhaps it's the lighthouse or . . . Why? Do you feel lost?"

"Yes, but I don't want to anymore."

"Is that why you wear a clock? Because you're lost?"

The only sound was the water.

"Perhaps it's the lighthouse or . . . ," Richard asked, but it took me a moment to remember the question.

"You," I said, and Richard Dorsey opened his eyes.

XVIII

Eel no longer asked me to join in his water games. It was a subtle transition, really, and I did not take the snub personally; instead, I would sit by the side of the pond and smile at my creatures as they splashed and flipped about, looking to me for the approbation I always offered. It was said to be an oversight, but I knew better. I could have been selfish, demanded their attention, but I didn't. I would instead swim alone late at night. I read alone. And eventually fell asleep beside only myself.

Had Richard Dorsey truly allowed himself to love me, my creatures' vituperative actions would not have affected me. I would have appreciated the space. But after our evening at the lighthouse for lost souls, Richard was again growing further away. I would lie in bed at night and wonder if my love—the love which I tried to plant so deeply every time we saw each other—was helping him find himself or grow more lost.

Days without Richard were being spent mainly in the Cactusarium, where, in his spare time, Dictator Cossman was amassing the requisite art collection to accompany his wealth. His collection was not world class, it would never be showcased in important museums or sold at auctions whose bidders were only permitted to spend their money via invitation. Cossman's art was primarily purchased from local galleries and museums. He always seemed to buy a piece not for its beauty, but its imitation of it. "If dimly lit, could one mistake this for a Schiele?" he would ask of an amateurish female nude. "That signature, why it looks similar to that of Rembrandt!" he would declare as he stared at handwritten scribble on a rough oil painted by a mediocre art student.

Often Cossman chose his art via phone, and I would be the one to retrieve it. I didn't mind this task, as it enabled me to be away from his roving eye. One day Cossman sent me to Rib County and a small art museum I had never before visited.

Rib was about twenty miles away, and I arrived just before dusk. If a museum could be dusty, this one was. Its walls were no longer white, and paintings hung crookedly.

"Hello. Is anyone here?" I called loudly.

There was no response, and I ventured into the main area.

A handful of mediocre oil paintings, a few sculptures, and a couple of drawings half-filled the dreary room. It was cold and there was a chilly breeze. My hair blew slightly to the left as I walked about.

I walked over to the first painting, the second, the third. Minutes passed. My hand grazed a sculpture of a hand; we were palm-to-palm.

"Hello," I repeated. "I'm here to pick up something for Dr. Cossman," I shouted loudly, but my echoes bounced off bad art and arrived again at my ears tenfold.

I decided to walk to the other room. This chamber was sky lit, but the sky was now dark. There were no lights. I vaguely saw a tag on one of the sculptures and moved closer. The tag read, "Save for Dr. Cossman." I held the figure to the sliver of dusk that hung from the skylight.

In contrast to most of Dr. Cossman's art, this piece was indescribably beautiful. It was a statue of a man whose features were slightly effeminate—the man's face was more pretty than handsome. The man was alone, but he carried a child's ball upon which the characteristics of the earth—the continents and the water—were clearly demarcated. It appeared as if the man had just caught the earth in his palm and was preparing to hurl it into the air. The planet balanced on the man's fingertips, and a clock rested at his feet. The expression on his face read scared.

The figure was remarkably heavy, but I could not determine its material.

I debated whether I should take the sculpture, as Dr. Cossman needed a showcase for a dinner party he was throwing that evening. I looked around. There was a closed door behind the sculpture room. I walked over and turned the knob; it opened. I heard men's voices, but they were so far away they were indiscernible. A long, dimly lit hall led to another room.

I quietly proceeded, statue in hand, until I reached the end of the hallway. There was a screen separating me from the area; I stared at gauze.

"I've been expecting you for days. Were you away?" It must have been the curator; his voice sounded musty, like the museum.

"Um, yes. I was away."

The voice sounded familiar. Astonished, I leaned closer. What would Richard be doing in the Rib County Auxiliary Art Museum?

"I figured as much. How were your travels?"

"The same as always, I guess." He sounded cheerless.

"Are you working on a residence in another location?" The curator was inquisitive, but not prodding. It was clear Richard disappeared on him, too.

"As a matter of fact, I am. I just returned a few hours ago."

I, too, had not seen or heard from Richard in days. If he was traveling for work, why hadn't he warned me that he would be gone?

"Good client?" the curator asked curiously.

"No. Too demanding, I guess." Richard continued, "Would you mind, um, giving me a moment with my new painting?"

"Oh, of course, Architect Dorsey."

"Mister." Richard paused. "I am no longer an architect." He said this sadly.

Silence hung in the air.

"The progression," Richard continued finally. "It's happening rather quickly, don't you think? I mean, the eyes, must they be so blue? They had been brown before."

"It's all according to your heart. It has nothing to do with the brush," the curator said.

"Yes, well. I cannot imagine my heart is dictating this. I don't feel it." Richard's tone was almost abrupt, somewhat abrasive. He had never used this tone with me; I wondered what could induce such a passionate response.

"Perhaps you are not allowing yourself to feel it. The paintings do not lie." The curator's tone was icy, an artist defending his work.

I was confused.

"Would you . . ." Richard stopped. "I'd like to look at it alone, if you don't mind. I want to compare it to the others."

"Of course, Mr. Dorsey."

I slithered against the wall, concerned that the curator would notice me on his way out. There must have been another door, for one slammed and no one passed by.

I shifted positions. An hour of strangled silence had passed, yet I had not heard even the slightest shift of position from Richard. Perhaps he had left? After a moment of deliberation, I decided to look around the screen.

Richard stood there silently. I could have walked back down the long hall to freedom, but something compelled me to watch him stand alone. Richard always looked different after his absences, and tonight was no exception. He appeared older and more distant.

In front of him, a wall showcased seven paintings. The first was of a woman. She was beautiful; Renaissance artists, Impressionists, Surrealists would have all been in agreement. Curly black hair, arched eyebrows, brown eyes, olive skin, chiseled cheekbones: All these individual traits came together to form a woman for whom the term *exotic* had been created.

On first blush, the second canvas was the same woman. Striking, vibrant, mysterious, but if you looked closely you could see that the woman was no longer herself. It was a subtle change, possibly attributable to a salon or a force as natural as the sun: The woman's hair was now streaked with blond.

She began to lose herself in the third painting. Her hair was straighter now, longer, blonder. Her eyes, too, were bigger, almost crescent shaped. They were less mysterious; their pupils were still brown, but they were now haloed in blue.

Blue haloes shrank brown, blond enveloped black, curls were pulled straight. The skin color faded, too; cocoa butter bleached to butter. Her little red mouth grew wider and her lips rosier. Collarbone, arms, neck, décolletage were all changing. Painting by painting, the woman was morphing into someone else. In painting seven, she was now unrecognizable as herself.

She was changing into me.

There was enough white wall for more paintings; conceivably enough to complete the transformation. Yet Richard did not anticipate the change; as a matter of fact, it was clear he didn't even want it to happen.

He stared at the first painting, the oil painting of her. His palm zigzagged down her curls, as if she were next to him and he was caressing her hair before they fell asleep. He dotted her eyelids with his fingertips; he touched his own lips then touched hers, as a lover may before hopping on a train for a long journey. His stares were eerie, his actions too intimate for an object of paint and canvas. It was almost as if Richard Dorsey believed the woman in the painting was real and would soon step out of her background and reciprocate his loving gestures.

"Where are you?" Richard Dorsey finally asked the painting.

She did not answer, though. Instead the woman's black, infinite pupils looked slightly to the left, at the paintings of the woman who was desperately trying to become her.

I spent the next twenty-one days trying to fall out of love with Richard Dorsey.

Days passed, but Richard did not attempt to contact me. I spent every moment convincing myself that life would somehow continue without the presence of Richard. I counted minutes and when that didn't work, I counted seconds. I counted down from the rest of my life—perhaps only sixtyish more years without him—and I counted up from the moment we had met. Every day was now lived toward one end: I desperately wanted to forget Richard Dorsey.

I soon discovered the only phenomenon that made my Richard-less hours pass more quickly was sleep. Therefore, I slept: in the hot afternoon sun, under the merciless moon, early in the mornings, late at night. My dreams were vivid and real, sometimes I would be afraid to wake up. In my dream life, Richard and I were always together, but something would always pull us apart. Often it would be a natural event—a meteorite shower or volcano eruption—but occasionally it would be a human phenomenon, sometimes it would be a thin piece of glass. It was never our choice, though, and oddly, it was never a painting of a woman.

Sixteen days after Richard Dorsey and I had separately visited the woman he loved, he sent me a letter. It was a cursory letter requesting my presence at the long-deserted Ix theme park. I fretted, of course, but ultimately decided that even ferris wheels and cotton candy would not provide enough exhilarating height or sticky sweetness to make Richard Dorsey love Zorka Carpenter. The hour came and went, and I felt strangely nonexhilarated. I imagined my lover at a deserted theme park, looking among roller coasters, hot dogs stands, Siamese twin shows, pistol games. Looking for, but never finding, me. Eventually, after many hours, I forced myself to stop wondering, and I fell asleep beside Octopus. That evening, I dreamt Richard's and my life had become one, and now it was frozen on a scary ride high above the earth. There was no one below, no one to save us. But it was okay because we had been looking all over for an excuse to escape the ground, and we had finally found it.

The next note arrived two days later and expressed concern, but I did not respond. Richard had awaited my arrival at the bumper cars, he said, and he was forced to ride them alone in circles. I instructed Raven to carry the letter far away, in order that I not be tempted to reread it and be tempted. Another letter arrived, then a phone call from Mr. Hamilton. I did not respond to either but instead repeated in my mind those words that had become my mantra: Zorka Carpenter will not love Richard Dorsey.

Kris Tina Woo was in Oslo now, she sent me the requisite post-card. "Zorka, I think it was a woman!" she wrote, and even her perfect penmanship had been excited. I read the postcard only once, and looked at its Norwegian monument. There were obvious mistakes and one of its walls was shattered.

That evening, the evening I received Kris Tina Woo's sixth post-card, I walked outside and looked at the stars. They were bright and I wondered if Heaven hid behind them, or perhaps Heaven was on their surfaces, or maybe Heaven was see-through and the stars illuminated it, too. I had spent the past 21 days praying to Mama—please help me do what you could not, help me accept the fact that the man I love does not love me—but she had not heard me. She was probably busy now, making up for all that lost time when she was on earth.

Instead, 21 days, 504 hours had passed, yet my love for Richard Dorsey was not going away. Indeed, it was that weird sort of love, the kind of love that grew even when it was given no sunlight or rain.

XIX

On the twenty-second night without Richard Dorsey, I ran out of sleep.

I knew this was a possibility. I had spent hours in slumber and my emotions were running out of storylines for my dreams. My creatures were tired of sleep, too; they would spend hours telling frightening bedtime stories, playing games in hushed tones. In the beginning, I would tell them to be quiet, lest they disturb my respite from sadness. Now, though, I allowed them to be awake and lively.

It was late, dark, and spooky, and my creatures were concerned when I left the house. A few volunteered to accompany me out, others begged me not to go, some were simply relieved for some peace from my heartbreak.

After much deliberation, my creatures decided they would not allow me to go alone to my destination; it was decided Owl would be my companion. He was not pleased with this task, but the night creature was the most logical choice since he was wide awake and could potentially intimidate potential predators. Therefore, Owl and I climbed into the car.

I did not know what I intended to accomplish. Perhaps the journey would allow me to find a vice I had previously overlooked, the single vice that would negate all our chemistry, all our time together, the single vice that would make me stop loving Richard Dorsey. Maybe I would finally find the rogue glass prism in Richard Dorsey's design.

"Where are we going?" Owl asked. "When will we be home?"

"We're going to . . ." I stopped. What would I say? Suddenly, the whole journey seemed like a silly waste of time. I contemplated making a U-turn. I looked at my watch.

Owl's bright, round eyes darted from tree to road sign to night to me. He was not accustomed to leaving the greenhouse.

Three hours before dawn—Owl's bedtime—we arrived at Dorsey Monument One. I stopped the car, and Owl rolled over in the back-seat.

It was pitch black, a pit filled my stomach. What if my journey to Dorsey Monument One had the opposite effect? What if its beauty caused me to become even more intrigued with its architect?

I climbed in the backseat. Owl rested on his side.

"We're here. I think you need some fresh air. Come on."

I opened the door and Owl climbed onto my shoulder. He wiped his yellow eyes and brushed his feathers with his claws.

Together, Owl and I walked toward the distant Monument. The night held wild stars and a golden moon, and the vast universe suddenly seemed too playful to be night. The Monument was remote and forgotten, yet the movement in the sky—its disorder—made everything around it seem alive. Owl looked at the chaotic sky and breathed it in, craning his head against mine. We approached. First, the Monument merely reflected the beauty that surrounded its higher floors: stars, moon, comets mirrored in glass. Then we moved closer, and stars and moon and comets disappeared into skyscraper. I looked again, even closer this time, and I was now looking at something else: A single skyscraper created long ago by a man who was supposed to be someone else. At this moment, standing at the edge of his first Monument, I understood: Richard Dorsey was meant to be Architect Dorsey. He was meant to travel the world, offering lectures and creating beauty which would never be torn down. He was meant to be in love and happy, married to a striking woman with black hair and piercing brown eyes. He was never meant to be remembered for jagged edges or to live in Unity, and he was never meant to be with a plain, lonely girl like me.

"Why are we here?" Owl's question punctured the silence. My mind paused to consider my response, but my feet continued toward the Monument.

"I think . . ." The Monument loomed nearer, and suddenly I was overcome with loneliness. "I think I am searching for a way out."

Owl looked at me with his wide eyes.

The Monument grew exponentially larger. I could see its serrated top.

"There was this day, a long time ago in Das Haus Retro, that I knew I should have left. I probably could have walked away then. It would have been difficult, but it would have been feasible."

Owl nodded, and I wondered if perhaps he understood.

"Now, it's too difficult, too complicated," I continued. The thirty-foot weeds covered most of the glass. "I just want to find a reason to walk away."

It was quiet for a moment, and Owl stared at the weeds. He picked one, and clawed its stem gently as if it were a rose.

"Perhaps you have found your reason, but you are looking to deny it."

Owl's eyes glistened in the lights of the sky as he picked at the thorny weed. Was there validity to that statement? Had I already been given a reason to walk away?

"Whooooooooooo?"

I looked over at Owl. He was alert, and his question was directed almost at the weeds.

"Whoooooooooooooo?" he repeated again, with urgency.

"What's the matter?" I looked at Owl, then the weeds. I heard a slight rustle, then the sound of a light rain. I looked to the sky. It was cloudless.

"Whoooooo?"

"Shhh," I said to Owl with kindness. I put my fingers over his beak to quiet him, and I stealthily walked through the overgrowth.

The trickle grew to a steady sprinkle, though the sky still twinkled clear. We headed in the direction of the rain. Water pattered on the weeds, dampening my hair and Owl's fur. The majestic Monument, however, was dry.

It was a few minutes before I saw the source of the water. It was not rain, but a human force which stood on a stepladder at least four stories in the air. His gray-blond hair blended in with the stars in the sky, and he held above him a giant sprinkling can.

The weeds were of myriad variety and particularly dense. In hindsight, I would have maintained that if one could have tried to plant such dense overgrowth, one could not have, but indeed, as I learned, these weeds were planted by a human hand. I stood beneath the weeds and felt the cool garden water on my eyelashes and the tips of my fingers and toes. I, like Dorsey Monument One, remained hidden for several minutes, which turned into an hour.

Finally, after much ado, many adjustments to the stepladder, and multiple sprinkling can refills, Richard Dorsey completed watering weeds around his architectural masterpiece. He struggled to close the ladder, his breath was deep and quick. He had packed up his belongings, but did not leave. Instead, he stared at the Monument, and I could not help but think that Richard Dorsey spent most of his life looking at the past, a past which would never be able to stare back.

It was then that I emerged.

"A girl I knew in high school used to say that there's a mistake." I looked at the Monument. A star bounced off the rogue prism, and I pointed at it: the prism, the star, and the mistake. "Right there, on the corner of floor ten."

Every tactic to avoid my eyes, Richard tried twice. He fidgeted with his sprinkling can, he glanced at the rogue prism. I could not read any response in Richard's face, as he would not allow me to see it.

"The architect was young then." The implication was not that the architect was old now, but that he had once been an architect. Richard nodded at my comment, but it was more head movement than an actual nod.

"How long have you known?" Richard's question was directed at the Monument, but I knew it was for me.

"Not in the beginning. It wasn't why I . . ." I almost completed the sentence *fell in love with you* but I didn't. "It was a mistake. That I found out, I mean. I didn't look for it."

The stars were so bright that Richard shielded his eyes. It was a gesture most would reserve for the midday hot desert sun.

"Would you have ever told me?"

"No." Richard still averted his eyes.

"Is this where you disappear to?" I asked.

"I go . . . I go to a different one." Richard touched the clock around his neck. I moved his fingers. The clock's black numerals read 6:34.

I was scared to ask another question, so I stood as the rest of the universe moved.

"This"—Richard motioned with his hands—"is one of the saddest things that could ever happen."

Water dripped off the edges of the dandelions.

"Sometimes," Richard continued. "Sometimes when we're beside each other, I look at you and forget."

"Forget what?"

"That I shouldn't bring you into a life of regret." Richard paused for a moment, and he gently caressed my hair as he stared at the sharp, jagged edge at the top.

"Things always end, Zorka."

Now I looked at the jagged edges, desperately seeing in them a beginning of the sky above, the stars, the Milky Way. Not an end to the structure below.

I touched Richard's face. I had missed this touch, and it again became the one thing in the world I could not live without.

"Just because something has the potential to bring you great happiness doesn't necessarily mean it will also bring you great sadness," I said to him, as little man-made raindrops fell off weeds.

Richard's bow-shaped lips gently grazed my neck. Raindrops fell from weeds and I clung to these words, desperately wanting to believe them, but for some reason I couldn't.

After I told Richard Dorsey I knew he was Richard Dorsey, something changed. Nothing changed within me, of course, but for Richard, well, it was as if his identity were a very heavy secret that, once revealed, allowed him to focus on his sadness, rather than the shroud of secrecy that surrounded it. Although I desperately wanted to know what catastrophe made Architect Dorsey become Mr. Dorsey, I never asked. The unfinished monuments, the oil painting of a woman: All were still part of a past which was not mine for the asking.

Richard still disappeared, of course, but in presence was more present. Before, even when we were on a blanket side-by-side, or together beneath the strobe of the secluded lighthouse, Richard always seemed far away. Milky Ways could have snuck between our touch, planets between our glances, years between the moments he grazed his lips on my eyes. But now, somehow, we were closer, if indescribably so.

Yet the first kiss of Richard Dorsey still eluded me. I dreamt of the kiss when I fell asleep at night; I imagined the feeling of it, the sound of it, the taste. Certainly, Richard was still interested in my intellect and conversation. Although my creatures tried to convince me that this was far more important than a simple kiss (which many called "overrated"), I did not believe them. When Richard even slightly tilted his head, I hoped it was to move his lips to mine.

Richard and I sat on a blanket in the foothills of the St. Pilara Mountains, eating tortillas and drinking a potent combination of fresh pomegranate juice, vodka, and crushed-up raspberries. The vodka seemed to baby-sit our insecurities for the evening, allowing us a chance to be alone. Richard's strong, tanned hand touched mine, and I felt a surge of electricity travel up my spine.

"Come here." Richard's tone was full of sweet mystery as he emptied the simple wicker picnic basket.

I heard its gurgle before I saw it. Moments later, in the moonlight, I could see the waterfall's splendor.

"I have a present for you," Richard continued. He held the empty picnic basket, and we both looked down the water. It was mesmerizing, particularly the sound. The crash of the water.

"God, I've never received a present before. Besides from Mama and Daddy, but they don't count."

"Now that's hard for me to believe. No boyfriend has ever bought you a present, Miss Carpenter?" Richard said this with staccato, as a child who is excited for Christmas morning.

"No, I've never had a boyfriend. Before you, I mean."

"How could an old man like me be the first boyfriend to a beautiful girl like you? You're just trying to make me feel better." Richard gently touched my face. How could the simplest human interaction be more beautiful than nature at its most magnificent?

"Better? I think it would make you feel worse that you got the girl that no one else wanted," I said. The sky was full of stars. It was as if there must have been a convention of sorts.

"No, no, no. It makes me feel very important . . . that I was the one who discovered you," Richard said lovingly.

"Marie Curie discovered radium, George Washington Carver discovered a thousand uses for the soybean, Einstein, the Theory of Relativity, Christopher Columbus, North America. And you discovered Zorka Claire Carpenter. I think you'll be in history books for that," I responded facetiously.

"I'll have chapters dedicated to me. Whole sections."

"Books, perhaps . . ."

"Semester-long classes . . ."

"Semester?" I joked.

"Okay, year."

"Better. Maybe even majors . . ."

"Doctorates . . ."

"Yes, Doctors of Richard Dorsey. Doctors of Richard Dorsey because of me." I laughed.

Richard turned serious. "Everything is because of you. See all that?" He gestured to the universe. "It's all because of you. It's all for you." He paused and reached for the palm of my hand and kissed it tenderly, as if it wasn't a palm at all but Bette Davis's eyelids or Ginger Rogers's toes. "Even the palms of your hands are beautiful. Each individual vein is a work of art. You're going to be needing these for your present."

"I still can't believe you have a present for me. I'm blushing." I was. A part of me hoped someday I would stop blushing, a part of me hoped I would spend the rest of my nights with rouge cheeks.

"This present is very special and you can't tell anyone else about it. Because no one knows it exists."

"Did you get it at one of your fancy design stores?"

"No. It's way too special for a store. Close your eyes." I obeyed.

Water gushed, burbled, and sang. "Okay, you can open them now," Richard said.

My palm sparkled. I looked closer. The same lines that Richard had so admired were now covered with a shiny powder.

"What is this?" I asked.

"Look to the sky and choose a star."

"Oh, I couldn't. There are so many."

"But, you have to," he said.

I looked at the sky. Although many people thought all stars—besides the sun, of course—looked the same, I did not. Some were coquettes, some businessmen, some belles of the ball, some brainy, some impish. Each of the little lights was its own personality, just as I was. Just as Richard was.

"Okay. That one, over there," I finally said. "She looks tired, as if she has been shining for too long and could use a nap."

"Put your palm to the sky and reach out as if to catch her."

She fell from the sky and directly into my palm. She was not star-shaped at all (rather quite oval), and she did not rest in my hand. She danced and, in her simplicity, was more splendid than the most ornate of chandeliers.

I looked to Richard. He was still more beautiful than the star; their beauty was universes apart.

"How did that . . . ?"

"It's shooting star dust. You can catch as many stars as you like with this, and you can keep them with you always." He looked at the star as he said this, then looked at me. I knew I paled by comparison. "You look so beautiful in her light," he finally said.

"But . . . I could never do this. She should be in the sky, with her friends. And, what if the sky runs out of stars?"

"The sky will never run out of stars. See, one already took her place. There is a line a mile long to shine in the sky; the sky cannot possibly showcase them all."

"Where did you get this?" I asked, as I looked at my powdered palm.

"That's my secret. Would you like to try again? How about that one?" He pointed to one of the most prominent stars in the sky.

"But if I take her, it could potentially ruin the Big Dipper. Look, she's a cornerstone," I responded.

"I promise you it won't, but you can always send her back if it does."

I gently placed the oval in the picnic basket, and held my hand to the sky again. The Big Dipper star fell into my hand. It was a perfect five-pointed star that even Kris Tina Woo would have been hard-pressed to duplicate. I looked to the sky and saw a star already in its place.

The ritual continued until I had a picnic basket full of stars. Ovals, trapezoids, squares, equilateral triangles, hearts, five-points, and four-points. I chose stars that were sleepy or villainous or wallflowers—stars with broken points or stars that had lost their shines in freak accidents or had never been born with them in the first place. Richard's stars, on the other hand, were of perfect design and illumination.

Standing hand-in-hand at the top of the waterfall, I felt sorry for Zoë Christie and Kris Tina Woo. They could never be as happy as I was now. It was impossible.

"They're so beautiful," I said to Richard finally, meaning the stars.

"They are," he said meditatively, while still tracing the thin creases in my palms. "Always think of me." He paused, long enough for me to believe this was what he had to say but then he finally continued, "when you look at them." Richard held my ribs very tight, as if he felt a star, far away, had shooting human dust and might pick me to join them in the sky. He then smiled that smile full of mystery that inevitably made me crumble. He looked at me, it was a look I had never seen. Not on him, not on anybody.

"Will you let me kiss you?" he asked politely, though he must have known I had waited for that question since the day we met.

My high school English teacher had once said that the most beautiful part of any relationship was the moment before the first kiss. It was after this that things fell apart, he claimed. You realized he had bad breath, his braces got caught in your lips, your teeth grated together like fingers on a chalkboard, but this was not so with Richard Dorsey. He was too old for braces, his breath smelled of freshly harvested raspberries, and the only things rubbing together were supposed to. The whole experience was so perfect, we did it again. And again. And again.

"Why would a girl like you want to be with a man like me? I'm old and I disappointed the world and . . ."

"And I?" I asked.

"You. You are everything I am not."

I thought back to the hours I spent looking in the mirror, fretting because I fell short of the woman in the painting whom Richard had loved before me. I reflected on Mama and the hours she spent waiting to forgive a man who was not supposed to be exonerated, at least not by us. I thought to the many months I waited for what had just happened, and the many months Richard had waited for the same thing. And, in that split second, under a full moon reflecting Richard Dorsey's eyes, I wondered why love could lie and get away with it.

XXI

Richard was fixated on seduction, but I am certain it was because he was just so good at it. When Richard looked at me, even the nerve endings in my ankles quivered, and I felt his smile in parts of my body that were under too many layers of clothes to see what was causing such a ruckus. I had lived with my body for twenty years, and somehow it was managing to baffle me more and more everyday. It was as if I were hooked up to an IV dripping sensations into me, even while I slept.

The dress code at the Esmerelda Lawn Bowling Park called for all white, and I was wearing a polka-dot dress. A sea of white golf shirts, white shorts, and white long dresses looked at me as if I were a threat to the society they had spent years creating. I probably was, as my blushing cheeks did little to refute this silent assertion and merely added to the unwanted colors I was bringing into their ivory world. Assuming that Richard did not know lawn bowling etiquette required such attire, I looked over at him. He, in his just-to-the-left-of-center creams, was laughing uncontrollably. Richard's sense of humor was whimsical, spontaneous, and impulsive; even if I did not find the cause of his laughter amusing, his smile was always contagious and his mere state of happiness caused the same feeling in me.

"You looked great out there," Richard said to me, as we walked on grass so pristine it resembled Astroturf. I assumed his compliment was sincere, as we had won in a landslide and, if nothing else, I was the youngest woman on the grass by at least fifty years.

"Thank you," I said, and even more blood swarmed to my cheeks. "So did you. And you are so good at lawn bowling."

Richard looked down and fingered a grass stain on his T-shirt.

"I'm not, really. I just practice a lot."

"You spend your free time lawn bowling?"

Richard and I were both chuckling loudly now, and our vociferous behavior was distracting the white amoebas discussing their lawn bowling games. I had spent my life as one of those unhappy souls. Now it was finally my turn to be in the popular group.

Richard stood behind me and put his arms around my ribs. He always did this really tight, as if trying to squeeze any remaining breath out of me.

"Um, can I ask you a question?"

His breath danced over my earlobes.

"Yes," I whispered back, still looking ahead.

"Would you be interested in coming over to watch some TV?"

"TV would be great."

And suddenly, I felt as if I were privy to a very important secret.

I am sure Richard's place of inhabitance reeked of style, but I did not notice. I could not tell you if the home's décor was modern or antique. I could not begin to guess its square footage, number of bathrooms, bedrooms, or sofas. If the rooms were painted, I could not provide you a color; if they were wallpapered, I would not know the print. I do not know if the home had a fireplace; if so, I could not tell you if it fired up gas or logs. Although I was sure Richard's fashionista circle spent many hours discussing it, Richard's design taste did not affect me.

It was only he who affected me. I absorbed only the home's finer details. I noticed Richard's fingerprints—thumb and two middle fingers—embedded on a liquor glass, and the orchids in the bathroom chosen for their snow white hue. Richard enjoyed books of architecture, fashion, and occasional fiction, and he preferred his Eight O'Clock Coffee extra dark. He was neat, as one would expect, but not meticulously so; he had forgotten to make his bed that morning and the outline of his head was still in his unfluffed pillow. He slept on the bed's right side, next to an alarm clock which read 12:04 A.M. Richard's aftershave, like him, smelled of fresh mint leaves.

This home was a museum of Richard Dorsey, and I was being allowed in after hours.

"Sit down," he said. "Make yourself comfortable. Do you want a drink?"

"Whatever you're having."

Richard escaped to the kitchen, and I was left alone. The air was still, and I was afraid to move my feet lest anything change the circumstances. I was in Richard's living room, and I wanted nothing to ruin this. I gazed down at a glass and chrome table. Hopefully, this expensive piece of metal was distorting my face. I looked like a cherub.

You're listening to Cool Jazz 103.

"Is this station okay?" Richard called from the kitchen. Ice cubes crackled. Liquid sizzled. Room temperature met cold.

"Perfect," I said. I was a jazz neophyte, but had once heard the genre was a precursor to seduction. An instrument, a French horn perhaps, bellowed out of hidden speakers. I suddenly felt as if this one-man orchestra was playing just for us. This was not a radio station at all, but a single musician live from the next room.

"I don't like to make all the decisions. If you have an opinion, speak up," Richard called. It was true. He hated to make decisions, particularly those pertaining to me. I would have made more of them, but I felt the mere decision to let him make the decisions was a decision. The top went on the liquor bottle. I looked at myself in the coffee table again.

Richard arrived with our drinks and I jumped up, startled.

"Hi," I said. "Nice table."

"Thanks, I hate talking about work. And I know it bores you. It has to. It bores me."

"What does your coffee table have to do with your job?"

"Oh yeah, I mean, thanks. It's eemz. I found it at my favorite store in the desert and thought it was kind of brilliant."

Zorka, *eemz* is not a word you're supposed to know.

"I could tell. Eemz is kind of great." I lied and stole his syntax in the same sentence. I had to tread water in his conversations relating to design.

"Yeah. Well, this thing is really kind of . . . nothing really." He took a gulp of his drink. Ice rattled.

"Cheers," he said, after he put the glass down.

"Oh, wait one second." I took a sip of my cocktail. "Cheers."

Thank God he went first. I had always thought you said "Cheers" before you sipped.

"Thank you for seeing me today."

Thank me? Why would he thank me?

"No, thank you. And, I don't get bored, you know, talking about your job. I think it's amazing that you're so great at something." I took a very unladylike slug of my drink. The heavy tumbler was sweaty, and I became obsessed with the horror of dropping the glass on the expensive carpet. I quickly placed it on the coffee table instead. Richard had not laid out a coaster, and this I found particularly refreshing.

"*Something* is right." I did not know how such a man could continuously deprecate himself. What if he had been a lesser individual?

We sat on the sofa next to each other, careful not to touch. It was sometimes unbelievable to me that we could be so whimsical at times, but so somber and awkward at others. We were like two couples; one married for twenty years and one on their first date to the ice cream parlor.

"So, you like eemz?" Richard asked. Ice rattled as he shifted positions. This was a safety subject for him, I could tell. I, on the other hand . . .

"Yeah, eemz is kind of brilliant," I answered. My ice rattled now.

"I think so too. I did, I mean, I helped a friend with his house last year and he has some kind of genius eemz stuff. Um. I'm sure it would bore you, but if you like eemz, maybe if you wouldn't find it too dull, you could come see it some time?"

"Eemz?" I asked. Those sentences had lost me at the first "I." They were a mélange of nouns, pronouns, verbs, and adjectives that had joined to form the words: Yes, I want to see you again.

"Now I'm not making any sense."

"You are," I said, and looked down at the eemz mirror.

A fat, funhouse face looked back at me.

"I just can't believe you're here." He put into a sentence what my mind could not even arrange into thought.

I took a long sip of my drink, the liquid burned a hole in my throat. The room was starting to look different; glamour was dizzying.

"Um, honey, I have something to tell you." Richard's words immediately brought my world into focus again. This was never good in books.

"Yes?" I felt my face wince, as if I were to be involved in a serious car accident.

"I don't know exactly how to tell you this. I haven't told anybody before, so it's probably going to sound a little strange. You see . . . you know those days I disappear . . ." Richard stopped.

"Yes?" I coaxed him on.

"Lie down next to me for a second," he continued, and positioned my body to adhere to his command. I stretched my long limbs to their limit and arched my back, all while he watched. Gravely. With intention.

His fingers dabbled in the little space between my collarbones, where my neck met the rest of me. It was as if the skin had evaporated, and he had direct path to my muscles and my bones and my organs. My insides were in knots.

I was so close to him I could see the gold crowns covering his back molars.

"How is your skin so soft?" he asked. He caressed the question's noun as if it were alive.

"It's your hands, not my skin," I offered in reply. I was convinced of this truth. I had nothing on him.

"No, I'm pretty certain it's your skin."

"I would bet all the money in the world that it's your hands," I said with conviction.

Richard's look should have been erotic, yet it was passion-filled and scary. His face was close to mine now, the closest it had ever been, and his eyes were little vacuums. My heart quivered, and the only thought on my mind was how to tear myself away from this unwanted . . . Unwanted what? Had I not wanted this?

I did not slide away. I did not slither away. I downright snapped away.

"I have to use the bathroom," I said as I headed away from the living room.

"It's down the other hall," Richard said. "Would you like me to show you?"

"No, thank you," I said as I made a rapid shift in direction.

I glanced over my shoulder. Richard was sliding his hands through his cropped hair, probably contemplating his stupidity for getting involved with a girl like me.

"Is there something wrong?" Richard asked kindly. A shadow had crept over his face and the lines on his forehead were prominent.

"No. No. Why?" I answered dumbly. My answer was particularly transparent as my eyes were glassy with the beginnings of a tear.

"Did I?" he began. Remorse was pumping through the vein on the side of his head. This vein was one of my favorites of Richard's many magnificent features, and its grievance made me even sadder.

This was my opportunity to tell him. Although nothing could be as disruptive as what had just transpired, it felt like atomic bombs were exploding in my head. He would understand. It was a simple admission, and one that every girl had to reveal once—only once—in her life. Richard, I have never done this before.

"Richard?" I said more as a question than the statement it was meant to be.

"Yes?" he answered, and his tone dripped of awkwardness, of sadness, of shame.

"It's getting late. Perhaps you should take me home."

"My allergies are so bad. I hate autumn," I said sniffling. My eyes were red and stung with tear salt. My dress hung crookedly now, but I did not care. It reminded me that there had been a part of the evening that went well.

Richard squeezed my hand softly. He was so good at paying attention to specific body parts. If he had kids, he would be the type of father who would never play favorites.

"Will you please tell me what's wrong?" he asked. Richard's permanent tan caused him to look serious, even when he wasn't. He was serious now, though, and I knew it.

"Nothing's the matter, sweetheart. I guess I'm just a little tired from lawn bowling, that's all," I said listlessly.

Pause.

"Sometimes I feel like I'm this old man and . . ."

"Shhh." I stopped him cold. "I had a wonderful time tonight, and I don't like it when you say you're too old because it makes me feel young and inexperienced." I desperately hoped Richard would pick up the inexperienced part, but he didn't. He just let it hang there. The evening had sapped both of us of emotion.

We drove in silence for the remainder of our short journey home.

Richard walked me to the door. Our footsteps grated against the dirt.

"Thank you," I said.

"I'm so lucky," he answered, and I did not understand how such a man could possibly believe that. But I think he did.

"Did you have something to tell me earlier?" I asked. "I think I may have interrupted you."

"Yes, I did. Um, I wanted to . . . I wanted to tell you . . ."

"Yes?" I asked in anticipation.

"You know, it really wasn't important. We'll talk about it some other time."

"Okay. To be continued . . ." I smiled.

"To be continued . . . ," he answered.

He got into his car. The car drove slowly down the sooty dirt road that I called driveway, and I watched it until it was well out of my sight.

XXII

In between his absences, Richard and I spent every moment together. On particularly windy days we flew kites (although such a task proved difficult, since we had to hold my creatures lest they fly away); on sunny days we went to the Ix Gardens; rainy days would find us dancing in puddles or watching the little droplets of water get caught on the Case Study ceiling. Although they would occasionally act jealous and vie for my affections, my creatures enjoyed their days with Richard. While the rest of my creatures frolicked in the Ix Garden's rhododendrons and lilacs, and drank raindrops, Tarantula would rest on the clock around Richard's neck. In the beginning of our relationship, Richard would try to move Tarantula. He would perch him on his shoulder, pet his little belly. But now Richard would place Tarantula on the antique gold clock, as if it were a place he belonged.

Those parts of life to which I should have been accustomed became new again. I would talk to Richard about my youth, and the words were fresh, alive, as if they had never once been spoken. I told Richard about Kris Tina, and we read together her postcards from

Dorsey Monument Eight. I would often ask Richard if he could show me his monuments someday. Richard would smile his sad, crooked smile, and I wondered if he was tired of his designs or did not have a valid passport or got sick on airplanes, for he would never promise anything back. Richard and I explored and learned together, and treasured our moments alone. A frog jumping from lily pad to lily pad, the simple beat in an old song on the radio, the way a bonsai tree grew more beautiful with age: There was nothing ordinary anymore.

Although Richard usually asked questions in order to avoid having to discuss his own life, he gradually began to offer up particles for me to nibble on. After much hesitation and more than a few qualifiers, Richard began to introduce me to his world of design and spent hours explaining architecture, telling me about the Modernists he so admired. I could not help but think how much smarter he was than Kris Tina Woo.

I learned never to ask Richard Dorsey about those days in between. He never talked about them; it was almost as if they had not occurred at all. In between Richard, I worked absentmindedly at the Cactusarium, tended to my creatures. I began to accept his disappearances as a part of the man with whom I was in love. I often thought of Mama's deathbed words and her belief that love cannot be defined or explained. Perhaps these quirks, disappearances, and whims were part of my love for Richard Dorsey as well.

In early autumn, Richard invited me to the big city. Despite its relative proximity, I had never been there before; Mama certainly would not have had the strength or will to make such a journey, and Daddy was a farm boy who would have complained about the city's traffic, congestion, and noise. I, on the other hand, read about booming metropolises in books and newspapers and was in awe of the brilliant people they had sent forth to the world. Richard told me to dress nicely—the place we were going demanded the finest attire.

I had decided on my black button-down dress and was primping in my bedroom (which may have been an architectural masterpiece but functionally was a disaster), when shouts and screams erupted from my creatures. I ran out of my bedroom to investigate.

My creatures held Ladybug in the air, as if she had just scored a winning goal. Termite kissed her on the top of her black head, and the air creatures encircled her like a halo. Ladybug had earned her first spot.

It had happened an hour ago, she said, for no reason at all. Yes, she had been particularly happy lately, though it was not a birthday, a holiday, or even the day of her first kiss. Ladybug was worried the spot was an apparition or a figment of her imagination, but my creatures assured her it was real. The spot was black, a perfect circle. Ladybug glowed with joy.

My creatures frolicked, danced, and sang in Ladybug's honor while I waited alone on the front porch for Richard. I thought back to the day, many years earlier, that I had found Ladybug. The Case Study House door opened then closed, and Tarantula labored down the cement step. "Are you going someplace dressy with Mr. Richard?" Tarantula asked, as he played with a pebble.

"Yes," I answered. Despite my efforts to the contrary, I sounded happy and I felt guilty. For happiness, for missing the celebration, for leaving my creatures.

"Oh," Tarantula said, as he scratched the pebble on the cement surface of the porch step.

I knew Tarantula well enough to understand that those two letters were not two letters at all.

"Are you upset . . ." I trailed off before I could exhale the words *with me.*

"I guess not, but sometimes we feel . . . we feel as if you're already gone."

"Gone? Gone where?" I asked.

"I should get inside," Tarantula said, changing the subject.

I nodded. "Don't get in too much trouble in there," I said and kissed him on his belly.

"Have fun with Mr. Richard," Tarantula said.

The air was sharp; it hurt just to breathe it. I looked down to the porch.

Carved in the cement were the letters ZC + RD in a big heart. The heart was punctured with an arrow, and the arrow's point was crooked.

The city was magical. Tall buildings stood side-by-side, forbidding the sunlight from reaching the streets below. Pedestrians skipped in these shadowed streets. All of this movement almost hurt my eyes, as they were used to the slow and deliberate pace of Unity. Unity was a town where people just sat and waited, the city was much different.

"I thought we'd go to Little Kenya for dinner. If that's okay with you, I mean," Richard added the last part quickly.

"As long as you like it. But what is Little Kenya?"

"Well, the city has different areas for different regions of the world. Chinatown, Koreatown, Thai Town, Little Italy, Little Kenya," Richard began. "I've never been to Little Kenya, but I think you'll like it. It's all outside and the food is good. And animals join you for dinner. A client went a few weeks ago and said he ate with a hippopotamus."

"Really?" I asked.

"Yes. But first we have to make a quick stop," he said.

The buildings were brick and stately, and their style and vast front yards were incongruous with the big city in which they resided. Richard led me to one with familiarity; when we entered the long, hygienic hall I realized the building's purpose. We were at a university.

Richard introduced me to Dr. Grandy and the Doctor reciprocated by expressing his keen desire to make my acquaintance in the wake of all the wonderful compliments Richard had lavished upon me. I blushed and averted my gaze to the far wall. An in-depth diagram of the domestic dog afforded me a spectacular view of his intestines, his stomach, even his pituitary gland. What a perfect creature!

"Ah, the domestic dog. Such a specimen," Dr. Grandy said. I thought I had been the only one to see such inner beauty in a creature most took at face value.

"You read my mind," I began, as I walked over to the diagram. "If you don't mind, could you take a moment to clarify something for me?" I asked.

"Of course," Dr. Grandy said. His words were kind and not condescending.

"I read many years ago that the domestic dog is an extremely close relative of the gray wolf, differing from it by at most 0.2 percent of mtDNA sequence. Is this a truth? And, if so, where do the differences lie?"

I had spent ten years searching for a response Dr. Grandy only had to pull from the tip of his tongue. He spent fourteen minutes discussing mtDNA sequences—not only of the domestic dog versus the gray wolf, but also of the domestic cat versus the tiger. Dr. Grandy then said he was the head of the Department of Veterinary Medicine at the college, and Richard had suggested we meet. Dr. Grandy would love for me to apply to his school for the second semester. They could use more students like me, he said, young men and women who were passionate about creatures.

"Oh, I am very flattered, but I couldn't possibly be a good candidate for your program." I blushed again and looked to Richard. "And I live in Unity."

"We offer extensive financial aid packages to our top students," Dr. Grandy began. "This covers tuition as well as room and board in the city. I would be honored if you would at least consider it."

"Of course she will," Richard said. He looked at me with silent support.

"Here's an application," Dr. Grandy said, as he placed a booklet in my hand. The cover featured a green lizard and I smiled. I wondered how my creatures were doing at home.

"Thank you," I said.

"No, thank you," Dr. Grandy said in return, and I took one last look at the classroom. It was shiny and well kept, and I could not help envying those students who were able to sit in it.

Little Kenya was the perfect choice for our meal. Richard and I ate stew, sipped on wine from African vineyards (who knew they existed?), and conversed with the giraffe that had joined us for dinner. Humidity—limited to Little Kenya, for the rest of the city had been dry and cool—sat heavily in the air between us.

Richard was always quiet, but uncharacteristically so at dinner.

"Thank you so much; this is really the best night of my life," I said.

The bamboo handle of Richard's fork rattled against his plate. I hoped he was not angry. "I don't believe that, but you're welcome. It was truly my pleasure."

Bamboo swept plate swept wood table. I had never been to such a nice restaurant before and was focused on my table manners. I hoped I was adhering to fine etiquette.

"So, do you have a big day at work tomorrow?" I asked.

Richard was silent. He looked at me closer now. Even the gnats and the wet air could not come between us.

"You are so incredible," he said finally.

"No." I looked down.

"How long did it take you to become so incredible? Was it a gradual thing?"

"Well, last time I looked in the mirror, I wasn't. So it must have been overnight." I smiled and my stare remained on my lap. Richard did not laugh, though. Did not even grin.

"That's hard for me to believe," he said, and he continued to eat his stew in silence, as if not contemplating something incredible at all, but something very, very sad.

XXIII

I did not seek Richard's past, but I found it nevertheless. The decrepit Sunset Theater had grown into its name quite nicely; in the center of Ix, it was the town joke, an eyesore. The Sunset typically featured old black-and-white films that had long ago collected dust and bad reviews.

I would attribute it to chance, accident, coincidence, except for what came after. Richard was dressed in a dark blue shirt, sunglasses, and his tightly belted blue jeans, and he slipped into the theater through the back, as if such a visit was commonplace or he was a very important person. He did not look around before the metal door slammed behind him. He did not expect to be followed. I strolled in the main entrance.

If the Sunset Theater had a distinguishing characteristic, it was its ceiling. A montage of dragons and Asian characters, the ceiling must have been quite outstanding in its day. The theater's other accessories—velvet curtains, torn high-backed chairs, oversized chandeliers—were just accents. It seemed wasteful for such a piece of art to be someplace no one went anymore.

"Ladies and gentlemen."

I looked around to discover the origin of the raspy bellow. It came from the back, from a projector room, from a furrowed old man. Besides him, we were the only two people in the theater; Richard sat in the front row, I in the back.

"As you are aware . . ." The old man paused, a pregnant and melodramatic moment. "Every Thursday we feature the same film. A film that needs no introduction."

Again, he paused. Richard stared straight ahead at the screen.

"So, without further ado, let us begin."

The sweeping, floor-length velvet curtains opened. The lights dimmed to nothingness, and an old projector sputtered, hummed, and then roared to life. The only light came from the projector and lint fluttered in its glow.

It was a gauzy black-and-white fade-in, and it took me a moment to recognize the face. He was a child, but even then his eyes led somewhere else: to other worlds, other universes, other lives. He sat on the carpeted floor in a living room full of sisters and toys. They could not hold his attention. He quickly grew tired of his miniature trucks, then he moved on to jacks. He tossed the red rubber ball into the air three times, and it became a soccer ball, then a basketball, then a magnifying glass, then a lightbulb, then a monster in hues of green. Each one of his passions was short-lived.

In his adolescence, Richard's life eerily began to resemble mine. In school he always sat in the front row and knew all the answers, but he never raised his hand. Like me, he stood alone at recess; like me, he was picked last. While my recesses had been spent playing with insects, his were spent tracing windows and looking at the sky. He would draw complex buildings on the playground asphalt—sometimes mansions, sometimes skyscrapers, the occasional church—and at the end of recess he would walk back into the school by himself.

The chalk blueprints would always disappear with the next morning's dew, but he was secretly pleased. Even then, it was his excuse to never finish.

His parents tried to understand him but didn't. He would draw buildings on his bedroom walls, and when the walls were full, on his ceilings. The sketches were too complicated for his parents; they encouraged him to join sports teams, find friends. They repainted and replastered, again and again wiping his walls clean. Eventually Richard grew tired of scribbling on his constrictive walls and in the middle of a hot Southern night left home to make his mark on the world.

His parents never looked for him. Not in the big city, where he decided to live, not even in the local parks. They did not file a police report, and though he would never admit it, he felt betrayed. There was a chasm between never loving and never understanding, and even then, Richard knew the difference.

He put himself through architecture school, where he was the center of attention, but his intelligence isolated him. He smoked cigarettes, he listened to sad music, he read fine literature, and he watched important films. His walls were still full of unfinished blueprints, ready for the world's accolades. He dressed in motorcycle jackets and his hair was spastic and spiraled, almost an outgrowth of his wiry frame and hopeful face.

Then the woman entered. She was a girl, nineteen, but even at such a young age seemed somehow older than her years. Something had sped up this woman's life, thrown it into fast forward, made it skip a few tracks. Somehow her presence managed to be electrifying, for the man in the front row moved to within inches of the screen.

They had met in the city. It was a chance meeting, really, over loud music at a club. Through his wordless gestures it was clear he was smitten; she was aloof and at once almost seemed bored, as if chance encounters were something that happened to her every day of the week. His gestures were barely recognizable as Richard's, but occasionally the flick of a little finger, the exaggerated lick of his lips reminded me that I was watching my lover fall in love with someone else.

They met again. A meeting which could have been chance had he not purposely sought her out. A party was the locale, a party in a seedy little apartment where he watched her from across the room. She watched him, too. Their gestures were deliberate, as applied as makeup. They finally neared each other and spoke. Their words were lost to in the clankety-clank of the projector, but they did not really matter.

Their rendezvous were different from ours; it was hard to believe that both would have been defined as love. He took her to real places, not to lighthouses for lost souls or fruit expressways or Little Kenya. They went to dinner; they socialized with friends; they listened to music, not waterfalls. They would go away together, to a little motel by mountains, and there they would swim late at night in the blackness. They would play water games, like my creatures often did, and he would hold her in the pool until her fingers looked like prunes and her eyes stung of chlorine. She was a journalist and Richard gave her an old-fashioned typewriter for her twentieth birthday. She lavished him with gifts, too. A drum set when he grew tired of silence, watercolors when he grew tired of his landscape. Neither of them ever gave each other stars, though they looked at them sometimes, when it was late at night and they made love.

Richard's seduction of her was effortless and quick. She was not fidgety or inexperienced as I was; instead she was adept and passionate. In the beginning, he would chase her around the room; as years went by, he began to chase her even farther. He wanted to get married, but she was successful now. Her articles were in newspapers and magazines about music and fashion. He painted with his watercolors; she bought him clay, and he made exotic-looking sculptures. He missed her when she was away.

Then he started to become famous—"the Architect"—and he spent hours alone designing his monuments. She watched him, handed him sharpened pencils, and kissed his neck when it was tired from looking down at complex plans for a wide-open future. He smiled at her a little—it was a straight smile then—and she smiled back. But her smile hid behind measurements and lines. He could not always see it beyond the distortion.

Faraway places called, and he answered. First Beijing, where he was greeted with bows and honors; then Iran, where he arrived to a hero's welcome more appropriate for the subjects of his war memorial than an unknown architect. In Cape Town, he was presented with a menagerie of Africa's best animals; in Riyadh, a jeweled crown. She did not follow him to these places. She did not want to stand behind him. Monuments passed, and she, too, decided to travel. While he designed his future with pencils and protractors and rulers, she designed hers with a map and a tape recorder. Their meetings were brief now, and while the world watched him he was trapped between a woman who had allowed him his fame, and the fame the woman so graciously allowed him. He looked ahead and behind. She only looked ahead.

In Oslo, he could not find her. In Iceland, he only received telegrams. Occasionally she sent him a copy of her articles, but all he wanted was her. The world was talking about him, but she was not. After Belize, he decided to go home and design his final monument; his greatest gift to her.

She did not come home often, but she bought him one. It was mostly glass and in the city. He sat there alone sometimes—oftentimes—and looked out the transparent walls at the city below wondering where she was. He sculpted for her, painted for her, dreamed for her, while she sculpted and painted her own dreams. He grew lonely in his glass house, and in those times he went to stores and looked at diamonds. Sometimes he tried to bring her there, too, but she never came.

More years went by, and she was really gone, but Richard chose to sit in the glass house alone. She came back every once in a while, with grandiose tales of the world and her success in life. Somehow life had managed to pass Richard by, though. All that waiting for something had caused him to miss the something he was waiting for. He could have left, but he did not. Instead, he chose to wait.

His face was tired and his blue eyes weary and his smile crooked. It was springtime when they first saw each other, one of the first glorious days. They met at the motel by the mountains, and Richard tried to entice her into the pool. He grabbed her wrists and when that didn't work, he pulled at her ankles. She shook her head no, and Richard looked to the bottom of the deep end where a diamond eternity band glistened. He looked at her again, but despite the newness of the season and the freshness of spring, there was nothing new or fresh in the air.

It was decided that he would be the one to move from the glass house. He packed his bags while she was far away, on an assignment, and took a final walk through their house before walking out the front door and closing it behind him.

————

The projector sputtered and the black-and-white faded to just black. The old man pulled the antique film from the projector. It snapped back in one last attempt to remain on the reel before the man put it in its obsolete metal case. There it would sleep until the following Thursday when Richard would again come to watch his past.

When Richard got up to leave, he did not notice the plain girl in the last row. He opened the grand door and, for just a moment, a burst of sunlight illuminated the back of the theater. The door closed heavily, light disappeared, and I sat in silence as janitors swept empty popcorn tubs from the floor. The heavy antique chandelier dimmed black, crystals no longer sat like little jewels on the velvet cushions of the seats. Even the ceilinged dragons were in bed for the night—or at least until the evening show—and I found in them comfort.

XXIV

I went home to bed. It was a brilliantly sunny day, but the sun seemed out of place in the sky. I closed my eyes, regret filling the blackness. I never should have volunteered to live in the Case Study House. I longed for a cement wall, a tiled roof, a wooden fence. I did not want to see the sun today.

I was alone. The other room was for my creatures, the rest of the world was for Richard Dorsey. I absently opened an animal book—*Essential Nutrition for Caged Tigers*—and thumbed to a page. The sun bleached the letters. My mind was a Hemingway novel; I glanced around, stream-of-consciousness, to find a distraction. The room sparkled. Kris Tina's thesis loomed like a bad cold, and I scribbled a few random, double-spaced notes. Sun. Escape. Miniblinds. Finally, I searched for my veterinary application. Perhaps Richard had been right; perhaps I should go to school. It was gone, though. Lost.

I closed my eyes and begged for sleep, lulling my mind by counting my creatures. I aligned them alphabetically—so as not to play favorites—and began with Aardvark, a reticent guy whose rocky relationship with Ant had initially caused dissension in the menagerie.

Many hours later I awoke to silence. It was rare that the pantheon was quiet; no flutters of the wings, no twitches of the antennae, no splashes of the fins. I looked through the ceiling. The sun had been replaced by blackness. Night had descended.

A few seconds later, I heard a noise and opened my eyes wide.

"Centipede?" I asked. "Millipede? Squirrel? Chameleon?"

"Shhh." Richard gently touched my arm, with a reverence far too respectful for an extraneous limb. "It's okay." I recoiled. His formal tone was in direct contrast to a gentleman who stopped by, unannounced, to wake his lover from a nap.

"Where are my creatures?"

"They're fine." Richard looked down, embarrassed. "I left you a note. I guess you didn't see it."

"No," I answered quietly.

"How are you?" he asked.

"Tired, I guess," I said flatly. "Would you mind if I napped for a few more hours? I'll call you when I am . . ."

No word could complete that sentence. Awake? Better? Resigned to the fact that you love someone else?

"Happier," I finally answered.

Richard rocked, ever so slightly, on the cement floor. He smiled a bit; but the smile was forced, as if someone had just said one-two-three cheese. I closed my eyes. Even the night seemed too bright.

Silence sat heavy for a moment.

"I went to Ix today," Richard said. He stated this as a doctor would give prognosis, a judge would pass verdict. It sounded final.

"That's nice."

"It was, actually."

"That's good."

"Would you like to know why?"

"No."

That should have been that. I had never been emphatic with him before, never turned him away, never expressed my dissatisfaction. This was the *no* of a girl who had lost her lover that afternoon and mistakenly thought she could sleep him off.

"That's a shame," Richard said.

"This whole thing kind of is." This seemed the most poetic thing to say, but I still loved him.

"A shame?" he asked.

"Yes. A shame."

"Do you know why I went to Ix?" He intended to take the conversation on a different course. His voice was sweet, sincere. I wished it hadn't been. I wanted him to make a mistake. A deadly one which would make me stop loving him.

"I don't know. I mean, I may know."

He cupped my head in his hands. I was still lying down in bed, with my afghan to my neck. He couldn't see most of me, but the look in his eyes said he was seeing all of me.

"I love you, Zorka."

It happened so fast that it was over too quickly.

"Was this? How do you know?" I stumbled.

"I had been suspecting it for quite some time, from the moment we met, actually. But, today, today, I guess . . ." He trailed off.

My outer smile was merely a tiny fraction of my inner smile.

"Is there anything you would like to say?" Richard's tone was once again formal.

"Um. Thank you?"

Richard thought for a moment. His next comment came out almost as a burst of air.

"By any chance, is there any way, you could love me, too?"

What a silly question. These words had flitted about my heart for so many months; they were now finally about to get a bit of air.

"I love you, Richard Edward Dorsey."

He smiled, almost out of surprise.

"Could you say it one more time?"

"Zorka Claire Carpenter loves Richard Edward Dorsey."

I whispered it until our names became one.

Richard ran; therefore, I ran to catch him. Ahead, there was life. I could see rainbows, the sway of wildflowers.

"Where are we going?" I asked.

Richard smiled his crooked smile. He motioned ahead.

"To the future," he said.

I first saw the castle on a hill in the distance, a medieval-looking manor with turrets and a large moat and a drawbridge with its own keeper. Even from far away I could see my creatures; my air creatures perched on the spiked roof, my water creatures swam in the moat, my land creatures played on the vast grounds. Stars illuminated the world, burning like lanterns.

My creatures were excited when I arrived, but they were also engrossed in their new world. I never allowed them out of the greenhouse together and they were giddy with freedom. Only Tarantula joined Richard and me, his furry legs grasping Richard's clock.

The drawbridge lowered, and Richard, Tarantula, and I walked across.

"It's so ornate," I said, as I looked around. The castle seemed the size of Unity and Ix combined, and its rooms were full of decadent furnishings and art. Long velvet curtains hung from black-ringed rods, and ornate chandeliers were illuminated by stars. Occasionally my creatures would scurry across the stone floors. I could hear the pitter-patter of their little feet and the giggles of their mischief.

I continued, "Did you design it?"

Richard looked down, embarrassed. "Yes. It's not my usual style, so . . . Well, I think it may be too obvious."

We looked at each other for a long time. So long, as a matter of fact, that I was worried we would use up the whole future in one stare.

"There's something . . . well, there's something I want to show you," Richard said, and he led me up the curved stone stairs. "It's nothing too great, though."

Richard led me through chamber after chamber, room after room, hall after hall. Finally we reached a tiny room that held a single, white orchid.

"I bought this for you. I hope you like orchids. I think they're . . ." Richard looked down, and he rubbed his shoe against the stone floor.

I thought back to Zoë Christie's locker.

"Erotic," I completed his sentence, and Richard smiled.

It was like smelling a flower and becoming so captivated by its scent that you forget the plant is of this earth. Although I had not realized it, I had spent twenty years living as one-half of a person, and now I was complete. Perhaps we were meant to have two heads of hair, four arms, and two hearts; perhaps we were not created to live as one person, but as two.

My Cricket chirped as Richard Dorsey slept. I thought how peaceful he looked. Occasionally in life, I had met people who were surrounded by storms. Mama had been one, as had Daddy. Thunder, lightning, monsoons, hurricanes had ravaged Richard Dorsey since the moment we had met, but now the weather around him finally seemed calm. More than anything in the world, I wished it were me that was causing the change, but I did not think so. Rather, I thought it was the sleep.

I grazed Richard's lips with mine and left Tarantula to rest on his antique clock. Richard did not stir.

It was a windy night, and the long curtains billowed in the breeze. I was shrouded in a thin, filmy white sheet; my shoulders and neck were bare to the warm swirl of the weather and my long hair blew behind me, back into the castle.

The formal balcony overlooked my past. Ahead of me, or behind me, in the far distance and beneath the stars were familiar places. The house I had lived in with Mama was decrepit, and pieces of the jungle gym were still strewn in the backyard, between old tires. I wondered who lived there, and hoped they were happier than I had been in the years I watched my Daddy leave and my Mama's heart break. Ix Public sat stately and wide; somewhere, there was another girl staring at a pantone brown locker and liking someone who was too far away to ever like her back. Even in night, the sky above Zoë Christie's architectural estate was still painted purple. Behind my childhood house, the trees of the forest stood erect, and I knew that between them, pronghorns played. Then, there were the monuments: The zigzagged edge of Dorsey Monument One briefly put the sky on hold; stone lions and crested gates guarded The Woo Residence; and the Case Study designed by the Woo's only protégée remained open, the wind its sole visitor. Richard's past was there, too: the Rib County Auxiliary Art Museum where his lovers hung side-by-side, the places he had been with her, the places he had been with me, the places he had designed.

The past was spread out before me, and Richard Dorsey was asleep in bed behind me. For the first time in my life, I found myself looking at every moment I had passed without regret or sadness. Instead, each place was a single event instrumental to my being here, here in a gilded future cloaked in velvet.

"Hey."

I turned around to the touch on my collarbone. Richard endowed my neck with a single kiss.

"Hi. Did I wake you?" I asked.

"No. I guess, well, I guess I just sensed you were gone and got worried."

I smiled. "I just wanted to take a moment to look at the view."

"It's magnificent, isn't it?" Richard paused. "It's strange to think that if even one of those events had been different, we wouldn't have been here."

I nodded, and we both looked out for a lost moment.

Richard held my hand and pointed my finger to Zoë's architectural estate, far in the distance. "I designed part of that house. The interior, I mean."

"Really?"

A sound of disgust was lodged in his throat. "It was kind of a terrible experience, actually. If I remember correctly, they had this daughter . . ." Richard shook his head, as if words were wasted on such a being. "Anyway, I eventually had to fire them. I actually kind of loved the girl's horse, though."

"I did, too." I said this quietly.

"What?"

"Nothing."

Richard still held my hand in his, and our hands together pointed very far away, into the distant reaches of the universe.

I looked at him with intent eyes.

"Is this where you go?"

"No," he said. "But, well, I don't know if you'd be interested, but . . ."

"Yes," I said.

X X V

My creatures loved the future. The next morning, they still busily chattered about the castle, its grounds, its views, and Mr. Richard. They wanted to relocate to the future on a more permanent basis. I shook my head and urged them to continue their lives. Richard's recent good-bye had been enigmatic and unsure, and I myself did not know if I would ever see the future again.

But the day after the future, two invitations arrived.

One arrived at dawn in the arms of a firefly. It was an invitation to the Annual Firefly Dinner Dance, to be held on the Twenty-fourth of December in the Meadows of Lophelia. The Event would commence when the sun fell beneath the earth, and it required the finest attire. My creatures, who were already energetic, were abuzz discussing orders of dance, dress, and escorts.

The second invitation, which was addressed solely to me, arrived an hour past dusk.

The letter had been sealed with wax and heat, as archaic etiquette would dictate, and my name and address were written in calligraphy with pure black ink. Even when I held the card up to the fluorescent greenhouse lights, I could not read its contents. Could this be how stylish boyfriends broke up with their girlfriends? Did Richard see the future and immediately want to change it? Perhaps it was classier to conduct such unfortunate business by post. Could I say I had never received the letter? Then I would be girlfriend to Richard Dorsey indefinitely, and I could protest at his future wedding because of a loophole.

I opened the seal reluctantly, knowing the contents were potentially life-changing.

The invitation was printed on heavy stock. Despite its brevity, I had to read the note twice to ensure I was reading the words correctly. The card read:

MISTER RICHARD EDWARD DORSEY

Requests the Honour of Your Presence

In the Year of 1959

Fourth of December

Nine o'Clock of the Morning Hours

Transportation to Be Provided

to

Lac La Belle

I wondered how such a meticulous invitation could have such a major typographical error. "The Year of 1959?"

Knowing I would not reach Richard, I prepared to meet him the next morning. I packed a shopping bag—I had never traveled before and did not own luggage—and gathered my creatures together. I briefly explained that I would be leaving them for a short while and assigned them each responsibilities. Just to ensure good cooperation, I promised extended curfew at the Firefly Dance if their behavior was good.

This did not, however, quell my apprehensions about the odd invitation I had received from Richard. As I lay in bed that evening, I could not even begin to contemplate falling asleep. Although our relationship was close to perfect when we were together, it still had gaping holes on those days in between. I could not comprehend how Richard could just turn off and on his emotions in the manner one would turn off a reading lamp before he went to sleep. Would this invitation explain the space between? Where were we really going? And would Richard Dorsey still love me when I visited his disappearances? In the end, the final question was the only one of consequence, and this was the one that would be definitively answered in the conundrum that was 1959.

The long black car with tinted windows arrived at precisely the ninth hour. The slightly ajar back door was the car's only invitation. Even my creatures were shaken by the peculiar events of the past twelve hours and begged me not to leave. I was well aware they had the brute strength to keep me in the greenhouse, so I quickly slid out the back door and into the car.

The limousine's glass windows were tinted, and I suddenly felt very important. Soon after, however, I quickly grew bored, as the black tint of the windows forbade me from surveying my surroundings and the window buttons appeared broken.

"Sir," I asked the driver's bowl cut, "do you know when we'll be arriving?"

"About forty-five minutes," the bowl cut mumbled back.

The limo finally pulled over, the door opened, and the view was spectacular. I had never traveled out of the state, but my unworldly opinion would still dictate that Lac La Belle was unequivocally the most beautiful creation in the world. The Lake was impressive in diameter, and waterfalls from the mountains kept its water fresh and clear. The sun reflected radiantly on its miniature whitecaps and reserved its brightest rays for this ethereal body of water. Fish, big as little sharks, swam in the Lake's waves, and turtles sunbathed on its shores. Yet there were no fishermen. It was silent, and I felt at once as if I was the only one to be let in on the secret that was this treasure.

"Sir," I called to the limousine. But it was gone.

I wandered around in silence for the next few minutes, expecting Richard to arrive. Perhaps his mode of transport was slower than my sleek limousine; perhaps he was detained by work matters. But after a half hour had crept away, I began to grow anxious. Maybe my creatures were right; I should have remained with them. I watched a precious water snake swim through the Lake. He was green, with friendly eyes. He slithered toward me as if on a mission, and I bent down to look at this prized specimen more closely.

"Hey, little guy," I said soothingly and touched his lean back.

The next thing was water. It was lukewarm, as bathwater that had been sitting for a few moments awaiting the tentative toe to take its temperature. The water was clear to the bottom, not seaweed green or polluted as most lakes are, and it stung my eyes. It was saltwater, I never wanted to come up for air.

The transition from Lac La Belle to the Year of 1959 was easy—I arrived dry and I was not bewildered, as one may expect after an early morning of time travel.

"Hey," Richard Dorsey said. "I've been expecting you for a long, long time."

XXVI

People drank milkshakes for breakfast in 1959. Not the diet kind, or the type with fruit and tomatoes, but old-fashioned chocolate ice cream milkshakes. As Richard and I shared ours at Stevie & Chrissie's Diner, I began to like this year.

"I hope your trip was okay. I wanted to come with you, but I had to do some stuff before you got here. I'm so embarrassed you had to drive in that horribly gaudy car. Are you all right? Do you need anything? Do you like the milkshake? Is chocolate your favorite flavor? I think milkshakes taste better in 1959. Don't you?"

Richard had reverted to his nervous habit: Questions. Lots of them.

"Yes. No. Yes. Yes. Yes."

"I thought so. So what do you want to do today?" Richard sipped his striped straw and cracked his knuckles. "I'm leaving it up to you. Thank you so much for coming, by the way. I haven't been here with someone, well, it seems like forever since I had company here."

"You know how much I love you," I began. I decided to start with the obvious to establish a benchmark. It backfired.

"God, I don't know how . . ."

I reached for my necklace (Foible Number 3) while formulating my response to Richard's blind comment.

My bead necklace had turned to a strand of white pearls.

My eyes followed to my T-shirt and jeans, which were now a chic white button-down blouse and accompanying capri pants. Black flats, rather than canvas sneakers, adorned my feet. I glanced up at Richard who was still sipping his milkshake.

"I'll be right back. I guess all that water must have . . . well, I'm going to run to the bathroom."

"Is there something wrong?" Richard asked.

"Potentially. Nothing to worry about though," I said and kissed Richard on the forehead. A million-dollar-red mark, in the shape of lips, tattooed his skin.

"Actually, very potentially."

"Well, don't be too long," he said.

"I won't," I said.

A stranger looked at me from the bathroom mirror, and I liked her. Certain features were the same—eyes, nose, hair color, physical stature—but my light blond hair was perfectly coiffed, held in place by a scarf of pure silk. My clothes screamed housewife-done-cleaning-drives-in-convertible-to-meet-husband-with-whom-she-will-have-sex-(quietly)-without-messing-up-her-hair. A dainty gold watch whispered 1959 time, and pearl earrings matched the necklace. I paused to decide if I needed to touch up the red lipstick covering my lips and Richard's forehead. Not yet.

I had to tear myself from the mirror in the bathroom.

"Hey, do you want anything else? I thought we could go to the hotel," Richard said when I returned. I wondered how he could be so indifferent about the fact that his girlfriend was now an ingénue. I had always thought "love is blind" was a figurative phrase.

"Richard, do I look different to you today?" I implored. The answer to this question was very important.

Richard held my hand as we walked out of Stevie & Chrissie's.

"A little tired, maybe. Have I told you how beautiful you are?" He always turned my questions to his. Yet another trait I admired.

"Not this year," I smiled.

"You are more beautiful than movie stars," Richard said, and the compliment lingered as we drove away in his DeSoto convertible.

Richard profusely apologized for the state of the Wild Yucca Motel before we even arrived. He was embarrassed by the motel's battery of weaknesses—"needs paint job," "broken pool heater," "rundown grounds"—and admitted his sole motivation for staying there was its flagship sign, which he considered "a kind of genius example of mid-century desert architecture." Fortunately, I was too absorbed in the one-two punch of Richard and my newfound glamour to try to keep up with that bold statement, and I found the sign to be rather rote when I finally saw it among a cluster of palms. The sign simply said "Wild Yucca Motel" in fifth grade cursive, and the words "Swim Pool" were written below it in similar penmanship. Richard's taste was funny sometimes. Perhaps this would explain why he kind of liked me.

Happiness surrounded me at check-in. I had never been on a vacation before, never been to a hotel before, never swum in a swim pool before, never looked beautiful before, and never been in love before. All of this was almost too much to take in at once; if Richard alone generally caused me to be short of breath, one can imagine the asthmatic effect this blissful combination had on my lungs. But Richard was impermeable to my euphoria, too intent on moving the plastic chair in our room a half an inch to its left to "improve the aesthetic of our space." While he made minor furniture adjustments, a tug-of-war was being played in my body. All these firsts in my life were happening in one day, and I almost felt as if there was not room in me to fit them all. My senses were full, the back-up parking lot was jammed, and there was even a line a mile long to get into lawn parking. If it wouldn't have ruined Richard's room rearrangement (the bed was on the other wall now), I would have jumped up and down in delight.

"So, what do you want to do today?" Richard's nerves had subsided.

"Well, first you have to explain this whole thing to me. Then, I don't know."

"Have to explain what?" Richard asked, knowing the answer.

"What do you think?"

"Okay," Richard began. "I know I owe you an explanation. But, well, we're going to be here for a while . . ."

My heart bounced around my organs like a pinball.

". . . so we'll have plenty of time for explanations. I'd much rather spend my first day with you, rather than explain why I'm here with you. Does that make sense? I can't believe you're here. Do you want to take a quick swim?"

"I don't know," I said, but quickly negated the response. It was the decision thing again. I did not want to irritate him, particularly now that *a while* was at stake. "I've never been in a swim pool before, but I didn't bring a bathing suit, so I don't think we can."

"I'm sure you have a bathing suit. No one comes to 1959 without a bathing suit," Richard said. "If not, we'll buy you one. But check in your luggage."

I picked up my leather suitcase. It was the chic brown kind with intertwined Ls and Vs written on it. I wondered if Richard had picked it out.

"Oh, I guess I do have one," I said. The skimpy little bottoms had a tag that said Givenchy and a circumference that said, "You're not getting your size ten hips into this piece of nylon."

"Maybe we should go to the park," I said.

"I can't believe you've never been in a pool. Let's do that," Richard said.

I slipped into my bikini, which fit as if to measure, and put on a terry cloth robe as I had seen starlets do in the movies. The robe had "Wild Yucca" written on its pocket, and I wondered if they would know if I took it as a token of my trip to 1959. I decided I would think about it.

The pool glistened, but Richard was a feast for the eyes. He was in his swim trunks, and I had full view of all of the rest of him. It was as if my eyes were racing around a field full of poppies and sunflowers and daisies and violets. I was certain Richard could feel my devotion all the way across the Wild Yucca pool area, so I turned away quickly and pretended to examine the intricacies of the white chaise. I felt as if looking at Richard in those swim trunks was similar to looking directly at the sun; you weren't supposed to do it, but your eyes wanted to anyway. Long exposure could result in blindness and/or permanent damage to the retina.

I avoided staring at Richard by focusing on the swim pool. It was a windy day, and little whitecaps interrupted the aqua blue surface. The wind died down for a moment, and I saw something flicker in the deep end. I wouldn't have looked twice, but for the instant memory. I heard Richard's feet—dull heels on hot concrete—coming closer, and I looked again. It was an eternity band. This was where he had been with her.

"That bikini looks great on you," Richard said with a smile.

Richard's beauty and the eternity band were blinding. I looked at neither.

"No, not at all. My body is so . . . put together wrong," I said. Perhaps the eternity band wasn't hers. Perhaps it was for me.

"Yeah. Those are the first words that come to mind." His response was a deadly mixture of sarcasm, irritation, and esteem. He stared at me with concentration now. It was that grade school game of who can stare longer without blinking. He wore sunglasses, so I knew he could win.

As I gazed into his sunglasses, I did not recognize the girl on whom they were so intensely focused. The sunglasses reflected an image of the girl I had become. The girl with set hair and big eyes and fancy clothes. I liked this girl, and I desperately wanted to be her for good, for real, not just 1959.

"Are you ready to dive in?" Richard asked.

"I thought you'd never ask," the girl in the sunglasses answered.

XXVII

Electricity did not come from outlets in 1959. It was generated by tall skinny windmills, the kind you read about in grade school Social Studies class and the kind that in the present were reserved for faraway countries like Denmark. Rows and rows of windmills sat like little gods on the flat strips of desert in 1959; in gusty combination with dry winds they powered ovens, street lamps, and black-and-white television sets.

"They're fascinating, aren't they?" Richard asked, sensing my awe. "They're almost seductive, the way they pull you in. Even after all these years, I still can't stop looking at them."

"I could stand here for hours. How long have you been coming here?" I asked. The question was benign, but Richard fidgeted.

"Thirteen years. I can't believe it's been so long." He answered pensively. "You know, I heard you can go to the top of that one over there." He pointed at a windmill at least fifty feet tall. "I've always wanted to go, but no one has ever wanted to go with me. Why don't we?"

"I think it would be scary. With all this wind . . ." I replied, but Richard was already heading to the windmill. This was thematic: I never had any choice but to follow him. It was all I wanted to do now.

"I don't know about this. I think I may be scared of heights. I've never been up this high before," I told Richard, as we climbed the circular staircase to the top of the fifty-footer.

"You'll be fine." Richard turned around to kiss me gently. He was like a child, and I knew there was no turning back.

"Oh my God. Oh my God. Oh my God." This echoed down the hollow cylinder and eventually reached my ears tenfold.

"What is it?" I asked, as I stepped up and joined him.

Oh my God was right. If that phrase was to be used only once, it would have been right then, on top of 1959. The windmill's perch offered the most spectacular vista I had ever seen. I could not believe that 1959 and the present existed on the same earth; it was such a pity an entire planet could fall into such disrepair. All around was beauty. Mountains crashed into the clouds. Rattlesnakes lived on the former, eagles on the latter, and strong winds molded different treasures. The swim pools and the hot dry air were paradoxes which never left 1959's citizens wishing for better weather, and the trees in 1959 grew crookedly and in abundance. One could have spent hours marveling at a simple piece of nature which people in the present took for granted (or, God forbid, cut down!). I gawked as if it were my first glimpse of the world, and I was experiencing it at twenty years old.

"It's so beautiful," I said after a long silence. This was a gross understatement.

"So, what else do you want to do today?" Richard smiled.

"All of it." I returned the grin and put my head on his shoulder. The wind was so forceful I felt as if it might knock us both off. I did not care.

"There are always tomorrows," Richard said, as he put his arms around my ribs. We stood in quiet. Stillness with Richard was so precious, far more beautiful than the vacuous, empty words that filled most people's conversation. I could not tear my eyes from him or my view. This was a postcard for 1959 and I was the girl in it.

"Honey, what is it you love about me?" Richard asked, startling me awake from my daydream.

This question was so easy I almost felt guilty answering it.

"Well, I love that bone, right here, in your hips," I said and touched it lightly. This was one of my favorite physical attributes of Richard's, and I had discovered it at the Wild Yucca swim pool. Having Richard Dorsey as my boyfriend was like a perpetual Easter egg hunt.

"You can do better than that. Go deeper."

"Hmmm," I exaggerated this. "Well, I love the way you look at me. Your stares pop blood vessels in my cheeks. See—" I pointed to my face. "That one was never so purple until the day I met you."

"Closer, but still not there." His tone managed to be both fanciful and stern.

"Let's see," I said. "How about the fact that I am standing on top of a fifty-foot windmill in a strange era, one which I shouldn't even be in. But somehow I've never felt safer. Is that better?"

"Acceptable." A little smile crept over his face. The entire face, not just the lips.

"Okay, your turn. What is it you love about me?" I asked.

"Well . . ." Richard scanned the panoramic view. Moments, never to be recaptured, slipped by. What was taking him so long?

"I guess . . . everything," he said finally.

"Can't you get more specific?" I asked. He could have just recycled, bestowed an old compliment. You have pretty blond hair. Your skin is soft like a baby's.

"I don't know what makes you love another person."

"But I can tell you what I love about you," I said.

"No you can't. A stranger could come up here and you could tell him that he has nice eyes . . ."

"But your eyes are the blue of forget-me-nots . . ."

"You could tell him that you like his voice . . ."

"But you speak in iambic pentameter, like Shakespeare . . ."

"You could tell him that he's beautiful . . ."

"But you are so beautiful, even time stops when she looks at you . . ."

"Shhh," Richard whispered in my ear, as we stole our last minute on top of the windmill. "Don't say that."

"You can't tell me what you love about me?" I asked, beset with alarm. I found myself growing light-headed; I could have blamed it on the height or the wind.

"No," Richard said, "I cannot."

Until the bright orange sun began to slide out of its place in the sky, I had briefly thought we had fooled night.

Richard and I had just been in the swim pool again, and I shivered in my white bathrobe. Richard insisted I take a short nap to prepare for the evening. I, however, had been resisting sleep in fear that I would wake up in the present.

"Why do I have to take a nap?" I protested. "We haven't had time to go to the stores."

Richard had informed me that everything in 1959 was much less expensive than in the present. It was not inflation adjusted; after-Thanksgiving sales were after-everyday sales in 1959.

"I don't want you to be tired for tonight. Besides, we have already swum in the swim pool, gone up a windmill, and eaten milkshakes, and it's only five. I don't want you to get greedy."

"You're right," I said, and sleep began to overwhelm me. The sheets in the Wild Yucca bed were crisp and probably expensive, the same bedding I used to dream of when I was a child.

"Will you stay here while I fall asleep?" I asked.

"Of course I will. Then I'm going to go sit by the swim pool and do some work. Okay?" His response provided reassurance. I would awake in 1959.

"Do you even have work in 1959?" I asked, amazed. Did his reputation span eras?

"I always have work." Richard paused for a moment and stared again. Right at my face. It was a long stare, with meaning.

"Who are you looking at?" I whispered flirtatiously, after seconds had flitted by.

"I was actually looking at that picture behind you. I think it's leaning a little over to the left," Richard answered, and embarrassment rushed to my face.

"Oh," I said and turned my head into the pillow. My face was so red I worried the cotton pillow would burst into flames.

"See, I can still make you blush," Richard said and giggled.

I was walking that gray line between wakefulness and sleep when I felt Richard kiss me in the small arch of my back. I shivered, as if a gust of cool air had just swept the room or a spoonful of cold ice cream was traveling down my throat.

I could hear Richard's footsteps as he approached the door to leave me alone to rest.

"Of course I was looking at you, love," he whispered to himself.

The door closed behind him, and I heard the footsteps grow quieter and quieter as he walked down the hall of the Wild Yucca.

XXVIII

The Wild Yucca was not to be our permanent home in 1959. Richard often talked about moving; he had been eager to move to someplace bigger and less transient for a long time, he said, but finally he had his excuse. He wanted to move to a real house by the mountains, away from the little motel close to the rocks and, I hoped, away from the memory of her.

Indeed, the enigma of 1959 was revealed to me slowly, as if each of its characteristics were a nibble of information to be chewed, savored, and fully digested before the next was spoon-fed. Richard would sometimes seem accustomed to the year—as if he almost took it for granted—but I was enthralled by Richard's world, and by the end of the evenings my eyes were strained from looking so closely and my toes hurt from hopping from destination to destination. Richard noticed this, of course, as despite our new era and the oldness of our love, he still watched me all the time, as if it were that day so long ago that we first met in Das Haus Retro. Richard latched on to my fascination with his world and offered me even more with which to be fascinated. We studied art together at night; in the mornings, we lawn bowled at the tip-top of 1959. Often, when we grew tired of newness and beauty, we sat on our favorite creaky bench by the swim pool and watched the mountains become mountains. We were giddy in those moments; "I am crazy for you," we would say, and we really meant it. I thought of Mama sometimes. The word *crazy* must have required an entire page in the dictionary, its meanings were so vast.

I could not tell you if I was in 1959 for days, for hours, for years. Time tripped over itself, and I wished it would stumble forever. Richard would ask me if I missed my creatures, and I would always say no—certainly, I wondered what they were doing and if they missed me, but Richard's world had quite nicely allowed me to free mine.

Richard rarely left me alone in 1959; he was often my shadow, following me from room to swim pool, bedroom to hallway. So I was therefore astonished when I awoke from my late afternoon nap to find him gone. Hours passed and I grew restless. I flipped through Richard's architecture magazines and hardback books, I walked to the swim pool and visited with the flamingos. I even asked the manager of the Wild Yucca if he knew Richard's whereabouts, but the response was negative.

Dusk was descending, and I was restless. I decided to venture into the town, though I rarely took the trip and certainly not without Richard. I scrawled a note and began my walk.

The town of 1959 was vast, but I had only frequented its downtown area. There a small general store and market, a barebones hardware store, a smattering of restaurants, and a few clothing stores all stood lonely. The Year of 1959 was more vacation destination than permanent destination, and the stores were reflective of this distinction. Shops only stocked skeletal necessities—flour, nails, and coffee, for example—and I often wondered if Richard intended for us to live here forever, or if we were eventually going to go back to the majestic castle of the future.

The townsfolk in 1959 were old. I could not imagine how schools, playgrounds, and Little League existed in such a place, nor could I foresee how 1959 would exist in thirty years when most of its citizens had died. It was a strange place, 1959 was, but I liked it.

Dusk was making room for night, and I scanned the village. There were few places Richard could be, and I considered the fact he may have escaped back to the present, but then I scolded myself for overreacting. He had only been gone for a few hours; perhaps he was working.

The toy store, the general store, the tropical store (sunblock and T-shirts were among its offerings), the small coffee shop: All were closing for the evening. I ended up in the town square alone.

I had been staring at the mountains for a few minutes when a young, pretty, pale-skinned girl came along. She chose to sit beside me.

"Are you new here?" Her tone was unaffected, and she fiddled intently with a diamond cross around her neck. I wondered if she possessed my nervous habit, or if the cross held for her particular significance.

"Yes. I think so. I mean, I lose track of time here." I smiled, grateful for camaraderie, for young life.

"We all do." She said this as she counted individual diamonds on her cross. "Where did you come from?"

I paused, pondering response. "Well, it's all very confusing, actually."

She nodded. "I understand. We have quite a few travelers from far away. It isn't that uncommon, really." She looked at the mountains. "The travelers, they're all enthralled by the mountains. Isn't that odd?"

I nodded.

"Why do you think that is?" she asked.

I thought for a moment. My eyes traveled up the long, spindly trunk of a palm tree, and I looked at the uneven hills behind it. They had always been this way. Mountains were the singular place on land that, despite every technology, humans could not inhabit. "I think," I answered, "it's their domination. We can climb them, we can stand at their peaks and look at the world from their eyes, but we can never live on them."

"Perhaps someday that will change," the girl said naïvely.

"No, I don't think so," I said with omniscience.

The girl nodded and her eyes twinkled. "Are you alone here? Or with someone?" she asked, changing the subject.

"I'm with . . . my boyfriend." I stopped, still reveling in the word. "We're staying at the Wild Yucca."

"Oh." Again, the girl's diamond cross commanded her attention. "Who is your boyfriend? Is it someone I may know?"

"I don't think so. He's just a visitor. Richard Dorsey is his name."

"Richard Dorsey, the architect."

Astonished, I looked at the girl. How did she know Richard Dorsey?

"His house, Dorsey Monument Nine, is quite beautiful. Everyone says it will make our town famous. But he has been working on it for so long . . ." She faded out and her lips moved, as if counting seconds. "People wonder if he will ever finish."

Dorsey Monument Nine was in 1959? I nodded, pretending I had been aware of this fact.

"I believe the Monument gives him a project, of sorts," I said.

The girl looked at me with glimmering eyes. "Well, perhaps now his impetus to finish has finally arrived."

I looked at her quizzically.

She sensed my confusion and she continued. "No one knows Architect Dorsey well, of course. He keeps to himself. But the rumor has always been that he is designing the residence for a woman."

"A woman?"

"Yes. It may be a fable, really. People here love to tell tales." She quieted, but it was clear she was one of those people. "Did you once buy him a glass house?"

I thought back to our meetings at Das Haus Retro and the Sunset Theater. It had been a noytra house, he had said, that a lover had bought him for a present.

I lied, via nod.

"Lore has it that Architect Dorsey is designing Monument Nine as a gift for the woman who broke his heart. He spends hours at the house, perfecting its angles and the roof . . ." The girl paused and shook her head, as if she was personally involved in construction. "He has redesigned the roof many times, and the landscaping, and . . . Well, I don't want to give any of this away. I am certain he'll want to show you himself."

"Most likely," I said. The girl's cross glistened as she moved it around the stars.

The girl lightly touched my arm. "You are very lucky," she said. "You will never break his heart again, will you?"

"No," I said, as I looked at the mountains, "I would never break Richard Dorsey's heart."

XXIX

Iarrived back at the Wild Yucca late, and Richard's face expressed
worry. "Where were you?" he asked, and before I could respond
he enveloped me in a hug that was so overwhelming I thought
he might squash me in his chest. I imagined ribs, organs all crumbling,
and Richard Dorsey once again being left alone with nothing.

When Richard allowed me freedom, I looked at him closely. His
face was still creased and intent, though it did not reflect anything else.
His clothes were pristine, his hair soot-free. If Richard had been working on Dorsey Monument Nine, he was covering it up well.

"Where were you, sweetheart?" Richard again asked.

"I had to go to town for something," I said with intentional mystery.
Richard did not flinch. "Did you walk? I would have driven you."

"Yes, well . . ." I paused. "I guess I was a little lonely."

"Sorry. I feel as if . . . Sometimes I feel as if I stifle you and I
should leave you alone." Richard looked down as he said this, and I
didn't understand why he would find such an admission embarrassing.

A toddler jumped into the Wild Yucca swim pool, and I heard a
splash. It was a warning, a subtle reminder that a diamond ring still
rested beneath the water.

"I like to be stifled." I did not heed the warning.

Richard leaned over and held my face, and I was once again scared to ask him the question I should have asked him for months, for almost a year. He kissed me passionately and deeply, and I marveled how everything about Richard Dorsey managed to once again feel new.

Thus, time passed and I never asked Richard about Dorsey Monument Nine.

I should have, of course, but instead fooled myself into believing that the longer I ingrained myself in the glorious world that was Richard's, the more I would become part of that world. I deluded myself into thinking that replacements could somehow take the place of originals, that a new love could eventually slip into the exact spot that held the old. Love, I erroneously thought, was like a jigsaw puzzle: There was only one piece that would fit, but any of us could morph into that exact piece if we tried hard enough.

Soon, I began to realize that each and every action in my life with Richard Dorsey had always been a calculated one, an unsuccessful attempt to make him forget. I knew I would never be exotically beautiful like the woman in the painting, so I self-deprecated; instead of making Richard sad, I made him eerily complacent. She was a journalist, I stood in the background; she left him, I clung. I allowed him to travel, not just to other continents, but other lifetimes, while she had walked away when he went too far. She became successful and famous, and I allowed him to brood over his failures. Zorka Carpenter was never good enough for Richard Dorsey, but she would not make him destroy his dreams. I deliriously believed that was all he wanted now: Someone who wouldn't cut off his life at the thirty-ninth floor.

He did love me, and here I convinced myself I was not delusional. I saw it in the most unobvious of places: the way he grabbed my ribs, for example; the manner in which he spoke my name, the way he buttered my morning toast, the difficulty he had in leaving me behind to go the grocery store. Yet in the obvious moments—those in which others' love screamed—I knew that Richard Dorsey was afraid I would become that woman. He did not want me to one day hang in a museum; he was too tired to design a Dorsey Monument Ten. In his hugs, I felt comfort; yet Richard's kisses were at times forced and even static, and his stares were often intentional diversions from the very woman at whom he was looking. Late at night, when we would lie in the Wild Yucca, Richard Dorsey sometimes listened to the palms, he occasionally listened to the crickets and the quiet splashes of the swim pool, but he often didn't listen to me.

Richard did not disappear anymore, but I often found dirt in his fingernails, and he always bathed as soon as he returned from work. There were minute cuts on his hands and feet, and although one might have attributed them to the desert cacti and the bitter winds, I knew they were cuts which could only be made from glass. He never offered a lie, though, because I never asked for one. Never did I ask him if there was a glass monument on the other side of town that he was designing for another woman.

My creatures, had they been present, would have asked why I stayed with a man who loved his past much more than he could ever love me. Sometimes, when I was alone in the swim pool and Richard Dorsey was busy designing the Monument, I would ask myself that question. I would beg the mountains and the stars and even the chlorine-filled water to offer me some sort of answer. As hard as I tried, though, the only answer I ever found was that a little bit of Richard Dorsey was better than none, and that I was very much Mama's daughter, always breathing on the life support of hope.

X X X

It was late afternoon, my favorite time in 1959. I was wobbly in my heeled sandals, and Richard insisted on holding my hand. I felt myself leaning on him more and more these days, and I was sure he could feel it, too. Even his arm muscles looked stronger.

"I think we have time before the movie," Richard said.

Nineteen fifty-nine was the only time he did not wear his gold clock around his neck. I looked at my watch—5:17.

"Time for what, darling?" I asked. I always called Richard *darling* in 1959; it seemed so sophisticated.

Richard did not respond, choosing to turn left. The gravel grated on the tires of the DeSoto; its dust flew into the open air of the convertible as we rounded the bend.

The tree and boulder park was probably more tree than boulder, although the boulders were more imposing. They almost seemed to swallow the gnarled trees. The trees were old men and women now, with hunched backs and bare branches hanging to the ground like walking canes. They understood that at one time they had been beautiful, but now they were dying. All were close to death yet unable to reproduce the life that would take their place.

It was silent as I looked around. Richard held his hand around my ribs again.

"Do you see the trees?" he asked.

"Yes." My answer was contemplative. "Can I touch one?"

Richard let go of me reluctantly. I walked over to one of the trees and touched its knotted branch. It crumbled in my hand. Dissolved to ash.

"What happened to them?" I asked, alarmed. "Why are they all dying? Where are their offspring?"

Richard did not come closer. "They're kind of beautiful, aren't they?" he asked, as he looked at them. A hawk flew down and perched on one of the trees, a twig snapped and fell to the earth. The hawk flew away dissatisfied, searching for life. "There was a fire here, and these are the remnants."

"But," I began, "where are the new trees, the new life?" I glanced around and my eyes began to tear.

Richard watched me more intently than ever. He appeared surprised at my reaction.

"Things don't grow in 1959, sweetheart," he said finally.

"What do you mean?"

"Well," he said as if he were a grammar school teacher teaching a child to read. "In the present, time moves forward; in 1959 it stops."

I looked at Richard's cropped hair; it had not grown a centimeter. I felt my fingernails, still short; looked at my skin, no tanner. I looked around terrified at the barren trees.

I smiled quickly. Richard glanced at me; his love for me was palpable, but he looked sad. I had last seen him like this in the Sunset Theater.

"They're really beautiful," I said quickly. "They'll stay beautiful forever."

But it was too late. Richard walked up to one of the trees, and he gently touched its frozen arm. It turned to ash.

The night was beautiful and dotted with stars and they blew through my hair. Richard and I attended the opening of *Some Like It Hot,* a movie Richard had been eager to view in the theaters of 1959 rather than see it on TV in the present. (These were instances when time travel was a bit confusing.) After the movie, we had been driving for about an hour and Richard had lapsed into silence. He always looked too serious, as if someone had zapped the frivolity out of him years ago.

We were miles away from the Wild Yucca when Richard finally pulled over to the side of the gravel road.

"We're here," he said, as a wake of dust from the gravel settled.

"We're where?" I said.

He had pulled over in a strip which had been, at one time, a little town. The village's main establishments were a Standard Station, a closed-up general store, and Duke's Tavern. Candy's Snack Shop boasted the "Best Home Cookin' This Side of the St. Pilaras," but I suspected Candy and her home cookin' had faded out somewhere around the time of the Civil War. The shack's roof had caved in and police tape surrounded the parking lot, instructing the odd bystander not to cross. Candy's was now a hard hat area. Save for the Standard, nothing was open in this remote place. The pretzeled trees with their long arthritic fingers and warped stems were about to overtake the town's few remnants. Nature was doing to this town as we had done to it.

Richard had stopped at the base of a mountain; directly above us sat a house. It was the most magnificent residence I had ever seen: glass walls, glass roof, glass steps reflected the moon and stars. Lamps were not necessary; the glow came from the giant lightbulb of the universe. Yet, as I had suspected, Dorsey Monument Nine was incomplete. Sheets of glass rested on the dirt ground, four different glass mailbox options stood side-by-side. Trees were merely twigs, probably planted and replanted and soon again to be uprooted. The Monument was not serrated, as were Richard Dorsey's other unfinished works. Instead, it was the only monument Richard hoped to one day complete.

Richard looked to the sky, the house, as if they were storytellers.

"I started coming here years ago. I don't really know how it happened. All of a sudden you wake up one day and everything about your life is different. It's not gradual or just a facet of your life, but there's a sudden change. And all at once you're different."

He stopped, as if he was absorbing this for the first time.

"I always thought she'd be there. Fame, money, commissions; they wouldn't be, but she would." He paused here. "I first went to Beijing, then Tehran. It was all very intoxicating."

I nodded.

"The monuments—One through Three, I mean—should have been done, but then I arrived at Cape Town. I sensed it then, there were crossed telegrams and gaps that had never been there before." Again, Richard looked at Dorsey Monument Nine. "I never finished any of the monuments. Instead, I returned home and waited."

I nodded. "How long did you wait?" I asked. The theater had shown the wait, but not its duration.

"Many years." Richard shook his head nostalgically. "I could have been someone."

It was the saddest thing I had ever heard someone say.

"Why her?" I asked.

Richard breathed deeply; this was a question that drove each and every action in his life. Yet his answer was surprising. "It's odd, really. She and I, we had been together for so long. And, you know when you've been with someone for so long and it's never easy and it never works right, but you don't want it to go away. And when it does, you look back and can't stop thinking about how great it was."

I could imagine.

"I think sometimes it wasn't so much her, but the idea of her," Richard said.

I thought to the Wild Yucca and the diamonds at the bottom of the swim pool. "Why do you keep her ring there?" I asked. "Do you think she'll ever say yes? Will she even come back?"

An owl rested on the Monument's partial roof. I closed my eyes, then he was gone.

"No, I don't." Richard paused. He looked again at Dorsey Monument Nine. "She's gone."

"Is that why you never finished your monuments?" I asked. "Because you can't end things?"

Richard answered, though not in words. I thought back to my childhood. Richard wasn't much different than Mama. Both were two people who believed that if they in their hearts kept something alive, it would never die. It did not matter that the object of their love had gone away. They defined themselves by the person they loved, not the person who loved them back.

Richard looked at me and he traced my fingers along the grapefruit scar on his forehead. I desperately wanted to know the depth of that scar or if it would ever go away.

"Zorka, love," Richard began. "We all have escapisms that confine us but also allow us to flee the very things that confine us." He paused, and for the first time I understood our age difference. The depth of his life. "I want you to let yours go."

"Will you finish it?" I asked. "If I stay here with you, will you finish the house?"

Richard continued to sweep my fingertips across his forehead.

"Whenever the house is basically done I find something wrong. I am now not happy with the master bedroom. Its lines . . ." He faded out.

My eyes teared and he looked away. I wanted a clock like he had, a clock which could keep me at the moment we had met forever and ever.

"Have there been others since her?" I finally asked.

"Yes. You." Richard said this as if I was enough, enough to sustain years of loneliness. And, just like that day a long time ago in Das Haus Retro, I wanted to savor this for a moment. Richard was quiet. Perhaps we were both savoring it.

"Am I the only one you've brought here? To 1959?"

"Yes. But watching you, with the trees . . ." Richard said. "Nineteen fifty-nine is an escape. It isn't a place to live."

"I want to be here with you, forever."

"Forever doesn't exist in 1959, sweetheart. Time stands still here. Dreams are never fulfilled. People never grow old together here. They're doomed to repeat the same year over and over. I know, because I've done it for many years now. I'll never get to 1960." Richard looked to the dashboard of his DeSoto. It was the 1959 model, in red.

"I want to repeat time with you," I said passionately. I was almost begging now.

"No, you don't."

"I do."

"I won't let you." Richard's command was directed at himself, not me at all.

"Please."

Richard squeezed my knuckles so intensely I felt them crack. I heard the snap of the bone distinctly, as if a large boulder had just fallen down the mountain. I wished it had. Perhaps it would have destroyed Dorsey Monument Nine.

"Can you leave this world? Be with me in the present?" I asked.

"I can't give up 1959. What if you leave, and I have no place to go?"

"But you won't need to come back. I love you."

"How do you know that?"

"I just know."

"So did she."

That *she* was so hot it could have set fire to Dorsey Monument Nine; it was so gusty it could have moved every star in the sky. Many, many years ago Richard Dorsey had left life on account of this *she,* and I wanted desperately to be the *her* that reintroduced him to life.

"You have to live, Zor. You're much too wonderful for 1959."

Richard did not speak to me during the ride back to the Wild Yucca. When we finally crawled into our bed, I felt the cool winds of the era singing us to sleep. Richard had his arm around me, and I thought of how frivolous seduction seemed in a time like this. Even with its nuances and intricacies, seducing someone was a hundred times easier than having them love you.

"Honey?" Richard and I were nose to nose, yet somehow his breath rolled down my spine. His stare scratched my eyeballs.

"Yes?"

"You have the most beautiful eyes," he said, repeating a compliment he had given me many times before.

"No, you have the most beautiful eyes. They're so blue," I said, and this I meant.

"But your eyes are young and hopeful," Richard said wistfully.

"And yours?"

"Mine, mine are not."

I did not reply and it was one of those moments in life when one is allowed a glimpse of the future before it happens. But the moment arrives just a little too late, because you can't save it, you can't rescue it, all you are able to do is watch it.

"I love you," Richard whispered, as if this were the deepest secret in the world.

"I know."

"Are you sure you know?"

"Yes."

"Will you say it again, so I know for sure?" He traced the veins in my hands, as a fortune-teller might.

"Richard Dorsey loves Zorka Carpenter."

"It even sounds beautiful. When you say it."

I nodded softly.

"How is your skin so soft?" He repeated something he had asked so long ago.

"It's not my skin, it's your hands."

It was, still.

"Promise me." Richard paused. "Promise me, that whatever happens, you'll know that it's because I am scared that I will love you too much. And not that I didn't love you enough."

And those were the last words Richard Dorsey spoke to me before I fell asleep.

I woke up at 1:15 alone. After a few minutes, I began to get worried. I turned on the light and searched our room. Richard's belongings were still there, but he was not.

I eventually found Richard at the swim pool. He was sitting by the pool in his damp swim trunks, shivering in the cool air that the night had brought with her. The pool was not lit, the sky was moonless, and the sole illumination came from the flamboyantly lighted letters of the Wild Yucca sign. The words "Swim Pool" reflected on its namesake, and Richard traced these words with his toes. He did this repeatedly and with concentration, as if he were learning cursive for the very first time. The water rippled slightly at this disturbance, and eventually settled back down when Richard relocated to a long white chaise.

In due course, the stately palm trees of 1959 fanned Richard dry. He lay on his back, parallel to the deep blue sky. Occasionally a garish and stray W or U would reflect in the whites of his eyes, and it was generally in these brief moments that his breath would switch its rhythm. It was many hours before Richard Dorsey felt compelled to look up to the window of our room. Satisfied with its blackness, he curled up and fell asleep.

Silently, I watched him until dawn when I finally returned to our room alone.

XXXII

Señorita . . ."

The knock on the door startled me from sleep.

"Yes?"

"I am sorry to disturb you, but I must clean the room for the next guests."

I went to the door and opened it a crack.

A maid, of about sixteen years old and dressed in black and white, stood at the door. She held a feather duster of real ostrich.

"I think your ride may be downstairs," the woman said.

I looked at the clock. It was 7:30 A.M.

Richard was gone. Style faux pas, or so Richard would have attested, once again pervaded the little motel room, and I was faux pas number one. I looked at myself in the mirror. My hair was long and stringy, the perfect accessory to my girl-next-door face. My fancy suitcase was gone, and a shopping bag held my extra pair of hand-me-down jeans.

"Do you mind giving me a couple minutes? I won't be long," I said, closing the door gently.

I felt like an uninvited guest at a dinner party.

I brushed my teeth, got dressed, and packed my travel kit quickly. I looked at the Wild Yucca bathrobe hanging on the hook behind the bathroom door. I hugged the robe close and hesitated. I smelled the robe, as if it were the last day of autumn and I had to carry the season's fragrance with me through a long winter.

"Sorry about that," I said to the maid, as I left the room. "I didn't know checkout was so early."

"Are you sure you have everything?" she said in response.

"Yes." I paused. "Oh, one more thing."

I went back into the room and approached the spacious window. I looked at the pool area. It was empty.

"I am ready," I said.

"They let you take the bathrobes with you as souvenirs. Would you like to get yours?" the maid asked kindly.

"No, thank you. I can't imagine it will fit in my bag."

I handed the maid my room key and walked down the long dark corridor to home.

XXXIII

The moment I arrived home, I knew something was wrong. Although the air outside my greenhouse was still, my intuition told me that the world inside was gravely amiss. I sprinted to the door and opened it. Disheveled creatures bounced off the glass. Birds with heavy wings were trapped in the fish pond. Bat and Owl were wide awake despite the early hour, and Snake hung upside down from the ceiling. Tarantula screamed and thrashed about in a web of seaweed, and Moth chewed on what remained of Katydid's antennae.

"What is going on here?" I yelled at the top of my lungs.

A hushed silence swept over the menagerie. Tarantula moaned quietly, and I headed over to untangle him from the green slime clinging to every hair on his body.

"I want an answer," I said. "If no one is going to answer me, then there will be no Firefly Dance." I was doing my best to get Tarantula out of the seaweed, but he was too violent. While I focused on him, my creatures focused on one another.

"I have to take Tarantula to the doctor," I told the kingdom. "While I'm gone, I suggest you talk amongst yourselves and figure out exactly what it is you want to tell me. I'm not kidding about the Fire-fly Dance."

The Ix Animal Hospital was open twenty-four hours, yet I had never had to visit the institution before, at any hour of the day. I had always prided myself on how well I handled and cared for my creatures, as none had even broken a wing under my watch and they were a happy bunch. "What's going on here?" the doctor said flippantly. He did not even introduce himself or say hello to Tarantula. Someone should have reported this man to the animal authorities.

"He's not behaving as usual. I found him trapped in this seaweed, and when I try to get him out, he starts thrashing about," I said.

Tarantula shrieked.

The doctor put his hand in Tarantula's cage and began unknotting him roughly. Tarantula was screaming even more loudly now, but the doctor did not seem to care.

"Honey, honey, it's okay," I said to Tarantula soothingly. "When we get home, we can pick out what you're going to wear to the Fire-fly Dance. Would you like that?" To the doctor, I said, "Would you please be gentler with him? He's obviously in a lot of pain."

"That is clear, young lady. I'm trying to get him out of these weeds so I can examine him."

"But you're hurting him," I said, while Tarantula cried in pain.

"I didn't get him into this mess in the first place," the doctor responded.

"Neither did I. He's sick," I said to the doctor.

"Someone allowed him to play with seaweed. And it surely wasn't me, since I've never seen this thing before."

Thing? I could not bear to see my Tarantula in any more pain, and I despised this popinjay who called himself a doctor.

"Get your hands off him. I'm taking him home."

"I would not advise you to do that," the doctor said with little venom or threat.

"I'll take that into consideration," I retorted.

And an angry girl and her gravely ill Tarantula huffed off into the darkness.

The next two days brought only sorrow. While Tarantula grew sicker and sicker, I grew sicker and sicker with want. I had not heard from Richard and hope made room for sadness. In my delusion, I thought Richard would come back. After all, he had vanished and reappeared many times before.

But as days passed, I began to think that Richard had never existed at all, that I was in love with a ghost. I did my best to convince myself that I had really been to 1959; I had really seen its twisted trees and swum in its swim pools. I forced myself to remember the sting of chlorine in my eyes, I tested myself on *Some Like It Hot* facts—Tony Curtis gave Marilyn Monroe a diamond necklace in order to earn her affections—and I even bought a chocolate milkshake to see if it was familiar to my taste buds. It was, although a milkshake with just one straw was not the same as one with two. I told myself that somewhere there was a white bathrobe hanging on the door of a motel called the Wild Yucca, and it smelled like the ecstatic combination of Richard and me and it had at one time made me beautiful.

My creatures were still out of sorts, too. Even under threat of cancellation of the Firefly Dance, they remained silent about the events of my absence. But I did not have the energy to blame them.

The night of my forty-seventh hour without Richard, I could not sleep. I walked out of the greenhouse alone, into the grassy flats behind my house, and thought back to the night when I met Termite.

My life was full of painful memories, and I no longer wanted to hide them or destroy them or turn my back on them. I chastised myself for watching life from the sidelines. Letting it pass by. I would not do it again. Not now. Not ever.

But now that I had finally decided to participate in my own life, the door was no longer open.

The drive to Richard's house seemed to take years, and once I arrived, I wished I could have taken the years back.

A tall metal fence of knitted barbed wire surrounded the decrepit building, barely recognizable as the house that had belonged to Richard Dorsey. A bright yellow sign prohibited trespassers—like me—from gawking at the eyesore lying among a field of waist-high weeds and overgrown trees. Trampled flowers—forget-me-nots— were ground into dirt. The cracks of the stone path to the door were dense with dandelions. Newspapers, mail, and coupons burst out of the mailbox and architecture magazines littered the street.

Undeterred by the sign's threat, I climbed the fence and approached the house. Paint peeled off the exterior, the door was unhinged, and many of the expensive windows were broken. There were no locks to fret over. Inside, the home seemed like it had not been lived in for years, maybe decades. Cobwebs hung from every crevice and a bone-chilling wind gusted through what had once been the living room. Furniture was turned on its side—some were covered with white sheets, others left exposed for mice's fodder. The orchids in the bathroom were dead, tinted with soot and ripped by insects. A rat lay on Richard's pillow, glancing occasionally at the alarm clock, which still read 12:04. Two liquor glasses sat heavily on the cracked coffee table.

The only bit of life in the house was the gas fireplace. Miraculously, fire burned on fake wood. Among gas and ash the third remaining copy of *Dorsey: The Unfinished Works* burned. Individual pages turned to dust: first Monument One, in the countryside; then the skyscraper in Beijing; then the War Memorial in Tehran. Cape Town, Riyadh, Oslo, Iceland, Belize fell into the past. The only monument that did not disintegrate into nothingness was Dorsey Monument Nine, Richard's sole residence and the only one of his monuments which had never been photographed.

I turned off the switch and closed my eyes.

I'd spent the past two days trying to convince myself that 1959 did exist, but this was foolish. It existed. Just not for me.

XXXIV

The next two days, I was deluged by a flood of postcards.

It was almost the end of her semester, the end to the allotted time for her thesis, and Kris Tina could not find Dorsey Monument Nine. She was "stumped," and peppered me with postcardal complaints. Kris Tina was skipping from city to city with agility, employing every conceivable method to locate the Monument, but to no avail.

The first postcard was from Calcutta. Kris Tina's prose reflected optimism (*I think I'm close!* she wrote). Her Indian tour continued with Bombay and New Delhi. Next was Japan, then China, then Singapore. Perhaps Richard Dorsey's final monument had been a bathhouse, a temple, an emperor's castle, but she was again wrong. After Asia was Africa. I knew Richard Dorsey had never been to Africa, but Kris Tina Woo did not. Game reserves, fortresses, apartheid prisons, the day geckoed trees of Madagascar: Kris Tina looked for Dorsey Monument Nine from every conceivable angle. Then she headed to Europe, where she visited countries like Portugal, Latvia, and Croatia. Again, she came up empty sighted and was exasperated. Her thesis and grade point both hinged on the elusive Monument; now she was B-bound and embarrassed.

Kris Tina had warned me this was to be her final postcard, and, sure enough, it was. Richard Dorsey had always loved warm weather and fanfare; wouldn't it have been ironic if he designed his final work in the bitterly cold and isolated continent of Antarctica? The girl had spent five days scouring the continent—she had a team of polar bears, scientists, and glacier specialists for assistance—yet she had once again emerged unsuccessful. According to Kris Tina Woo, Doctor of Richard Dorsey, there had never been a Dorsey Monument Nine.

I was reading Kris Tina's postcards for the twenty-seventh time when the phone rang. I still naïvely hoped the caller would be Richard. I cursed myself for this hope and willed it to stop.

The phone's shrill was earshattering, but I merely allowed it to ring. It would eventually stop, I thought. Things always went away.

But the phone was as persistent as a 911 call. "Can somebody please answer that?" I called.

A few moments later, Dove sailed into my room with the phone in her beak. She glanced at me with pity, almost nonrecognition, and I thought about Mama after her heart had cracked down the middle. I was not going to be her.

"Thank you," I said to Dove.

"Hello?" I said into the phone.

"Well, hello there, Zorka."

The voice was vaguely familiar.

"Hello?"

"This is Dr. Grandy, from the veterinary school. I made your acquaintance through Richard Dorsey."

"Of course. How are you, Doctor?" Richard's name was still so harmonious. Did it sound so musical to Dr. Grandy?

"I'm quite well, thank you for inquiring. I do not wish to detain you, but I am just calling personally to express our gratitude for your application, as well as to inform you that you have been accepted to our January program. We are thrilled that you are interested in joining us in the city."

Program? Application? Accepted?

"There must be some mistake." I had never applied to veterinary school.

"No, there is no mistake, Zorka. You were one of our strongest applicants. Dr. Weber—who teaches Domestication of Wildlife—said that in his twenty-three years on the admissions board he had never been so moved by an entrance essay. And I have to agree. Our faculty is very eager to meet you, Zorka."

"My essay?"

"Yes. Your brilliant third-person essay about the twinkle in your eye when you look at a rattlesnake. It brought goose bumps to the staff. Really. It was almost as if it was written not by you at all, but . . ." He trailed off. "Never mind. I tend to be tangential. You'll notice that very quickly when you start my anatomy class."

I stared at the sun, and I hugged myself tightly. I saw my reflection in Dove's jet-black eyes, but it was a very different reflection than I had once observed in Richard's sunglasses. Dr. Grandy was still talking, I think, but I could not even muster an "um," an "oh," a "thank you." I simply did not know what to say.

It was rare to find my creatures silent. I was still not accustomed to seeing Ladybug with her spot; she rested beside Black Widow who was caressing her dotted shell. Had Millipede stepped forward, had Tuna inhaled deeply, had Bat blinked an eyelash, the sound would have been heard for miles.

It was I who sliced the stillness.

"I just received a phone call," I began, hoping to solicit a reaction. Creature looked at creature. "A very important document has disappeared from my bedroom."

Wings did not flutter. Fins did not swim. Antennae did not twitch.

"Do you know what may have happened to it?" I continued, studying my creatures.

Beady eyes did not move. Insect legs did not leave cement.

I felt miles away from my creatures. They were in front of me, of course, attentive and understanding, waiting as always. But something was different, as if the glass walls of the Case Study House had been reengineered. An ornate spider web separated me from the creatures I so adored. They were no longer submissive.

"Okay." I nodded, resigned. I retreated to my bedroom and closed the door to my creatures' quarters more firmly than necessary.

I heard a collective sigh, as wings once again fluttered, fins swam, antennae twitched, beady eyes moved, and insect legs left cement.

XXXV

Tarantula no longer had eight legs, a full set of teeth, or two antennae. He was losing his hair, and could not go a moment without writhing in pain. He screamed for an end. Tarantula was dying. I could not reverse death, I had mistakenly thought—not of a creature, not of a person, not of love. I accepted this until I received the January issue of *Scientific Creatures,* an installment dedicated to mating.

According to *Scientific Creatures,* the mature male tarantula was solely focused on what he considered to be his one true life purpose, mating. Tarantulas had a very short mature life span, and they attempted to procreate as soon as they were mature. Due to this genetic disposition, male tarantulas could not, under any circumstances, be kept in captivity, for they would literally tear themselves to pieces trying to find a female to continue their lifeblood. This was Tarantula's fate.

Despite their poor behavior, I planned to allow my entire family to attend the Fourth Annual Firefly Dinner Dance, a decision greeted by cheers from the whole menagerie. Ladybug tried on a floor-length gown; Cricket and Seahorse, tuxes with tails; and Snake, the latest in bowties. Hawk discussed possible escorts, and the voting began for Firefly King and Queen. Fireflies flitted with gold and silver decorations; candles, flowers, and tents graced the Meadows of Lophelia. This was expected to be the most extravagant Firefly Dinner Dance ever. I was hero to all my creatures, and there were mumblings that I was going to sit at the Queen's table with silver goblets and lace napkins.

Life after Richard was far bleaker than life before. I skated through my days, finding myself eager to tell him about little life events ("Baby Shark lost his first tooth today!") and, more important, the life-changing ones which were to occur the night of the Firefly Dance. I often wondered if he thought of me.

I felt the ache of Richard's absence most acutely at the Cactusarium. For many years life there had been grim, but over the past months I had grown accustomed to Richard's presence, his soothing voice, his sense of humor. As days went by and I gradually began to accept that Richard was no longer waiting for me at the end of my shift, the Cactusarium grew unbearable.

I was reading *The Grapes of Wrath* to four of the cacti when it happened.

" 'The owners of the land came onto the land, or more often a spokesman for the owners came. They came in closed cars, and they felt the dry earth with their fingers, and sometimes they drove big earth . . . ' "

"I want you in my office now!" Cossman interrupted.

"Yes, Doctor," I replied, setting the book on the stones at my feet. The cacti glanced at one another with concern.

"What is this I hear about you not showing up to your shifts?"

"I was called out of town unexpectedly, sir," I began with a touch of pride. *Out of town* was so enigmatic, and *unexpectedly* so important. "But Jesse volunteered to pick up my hours, so he filled in. See . . ." I pointed to a timecard on the wall.

"Where would anyone call *you* to unexpectedly?" Cossman asked.

"My boyfriend invited me to . . . ," I began.

"A boyfriend?" Cossman threw out the word maliciously. "The words *boyfriend* and *Zorka Carpenter* hardly belong in the same sentence. . . ." Cossman turned to me. "From now on, I don't want you getting substitutes on shifts. Do you understand?"

"Yes," I replied, and walked back into the park.

I picked up Steinbeck, but Cossman's words lingered cold in my heart. He was right: Richard Dorsey may have never loved me. On the windmill in 1959, in an entire encyclopedia of compliments, he could not find one to describe his love for me. Perhaps I was an experiment; maybe I was like the bowling shoe, the chain wallet, the skull cap. Maybe Richard just wanted to prove he could carry me off.

Skimming *The Grapes of Wrath,* I scrutinized the cacti. We are drawn to the familiar, and the familiar had drawn me to the Cactusarium. Cacti were docile, introverted, passive creatures. I had once been that, too. But I had been a girl then, and now I was something else.

"Don't you ever knock?" Cossman barked when I entered his office unannounced. "What is so important that it can't wait until tomorrow?"

"It's actually about my shift tomorrow, Dr. Cossman," I began. "I am not going to be here."

"Did you not hear anything I just said?"

"I did. And I have something to tell you, Dictator. You're a mean, money-hungry man who doesn't care about these beautiful plants or your employees. All you care about is turning nature against itself for profit. And I won't work for someone like that."

Cossman was speechless, and I slammed the door as I left.

XXXVI

The day of the Firefly Dinner Dance arrived quietly. When I awoke, each of my creatures were fast asleep in anticipation of the joyful evening. Before I left to make my hourlong journey, I kissed every one on the tops of their heads. Some stirred, others remained in deep slumber.

Only Owl awoke. "Whoooooooo?" he asked.

"Yes, I love youuuuu," I answered with tears in my eyes.

He smiled and fell back to sleep.

Das Haus Retro looked different. It was not its paint, which still glistened silver; it was not its parking lot, which was still full of European-made sports cars; it was not its clientele, who were still design types in constant turmoil over the next hip-old-thing.

"Hello, there," Hamilton greeted me at the door.

"Hello, Mr. Hamilton," I responded, and tried to meander past him to the aluminum cleaner aisle. I wanted to leave the store as quickly as possible.

"No need to go in there," Hamilton continued, stopping me in my tracks. "We no longer carry Xall Xoff. Stopped a few days ago. I found that it wasn't working for my more discriminate buyers, just for . . ."

The glimmering world of a bygone age was arranged according to aisle in Das Haus Retro. Hamilton was the gatekeeper, and he had changed the password.

"Well, you must carry aluminum cleaners. I really need one by to-night, so could I just sneak through? That's all I need. I'll be out in a minute."

Behind Hamilton, I saw a woman. She was laughing in the '50s aisle at a joke I could not hear and probably would not have understood even if I had. The woman threw her head back exaggeratedly and tossed her radiant grin to the handsome design-type who stood beside her. I was sure this woman lived in a real glass house, not a greenhouse full of bugs, birds, and fish, and she had every right to be in Das Haus Retro looking for aluminum cleaners. She could afford them, she knew how to apply them, she could probably even read the instructions in their native German. She was Das Haus Retro's target market.

I did not hesitate when I made my decision. I would leave the way I always wanted to. With dignity.

"Actually, you're right. I'll head someplace else to look for a cleaner. I'm sure it's not difficult to find," I said and turned toward the doors.

Hamilton's tone turned friendlier.

"You may want to check Hal's Hardware. I think they have a decent one," he said.

"Thank you. It's on my way home, so I'll try that," I declared.

I looked back at the store, its perfectly ordered aisles, its shiny cement floor, its optimism.

"Good luck, Mr. Hamilton," I said.

And behind me, the electronic doors melded together in a perfect glass square.

XXXVII

It was mating season, and Grasshopper was getting frisky. At first I thought his abrupt change in behavior was the direct result of daylight saving time, a twice-yearly ritual which temporarily wreacked havoc on the entire menagerie. Yet, despite its lofty status as the most powerful object in nature's kingdom, the sun did not have the clout to make tarantulas tear themselves to death, to make grasshoppers self-destructively flail against glass, to make a woman die of loneliness. The sun, even in all its glory, did not have the authority to break my heart.

I held my head high as my creatures exited the greenhouse, in single file procession to the Annual Firefly Dinner Dance. I had 310 sons and daughters, and, for the first time in the history of the Firefly Dance, I insisted on inspecting them individually as they left our glass home. The creatures had reluctantly lined up, like little soldiers ready for battle.

The first creature in line was Millipede.

"I think you have an unfair advantage, Millipede. Of course, you're going to be first in line with all those legs," I said.

Millipede laughed and looked back for a moment, as if he thought I would make him go to the end of the line.

"I'm kidding," I said. "You look great. Have fun tonight."

Ladybug was next.

"Who is this beautiful girl?" I asked, winking. Ladybug blushed, bright red, and it reminded me of me when I had been around Richard.

"Behave yourself, and remember to play hard-to-get. Okay?"

Ladybug nodded and sashayed in Millipede's tracks.

Then came Jellyfish.

"Hey, hey good-looking," I said. "Who's your date to the big party tonight?"

"A beautiflical jellyfish from Ikis," Jellyfish said. Nerves and excitement made his speech impediment even more pronounced tonight.

"Well, she is one lucky girl," I said.

Next was Bat, looking particularly handsome in his tux.

"Look at you, Bat!" I said. "You're going to be such a handsome guy when you grow up, a regular heartbreaker."

"I would never break a heart," Bat said genuinely.

Bat would keep me company late at night when I could not sleep because of Richard. He knew more about my life than almost any of my creatures.

"I know you wouldn't, honey. You know I will always think of you late at night, don't you?" I asked him.

"Yes, because you're my night friend."

"I'll always be your night friend, Bat," I replied sadly.

The ritual was much the same for all of my creatures. Despite the large size of my family, I had memories with every one of them, and I loved them all. They were so beautiful, my creatures, and I had been so lucky to have them.

There were only two creatures left now.

"Hi, Termite," I said. I had been composed but now tears filled my eyes. I forced them back in.

"What's wrong?" he asked.

"Nothing, baby. I just can't believe how grown up you look. Can you believe how long we've known each other?"

"I've been so happy since I met you," Termite replied.

My throat was choked with tears now.

"I wanted to tell you that . . . that night of Mama's funeral . . . I'm glad you came home from the forest with me," I began.

"I didn't even know if antlers were predominantly used for mating purposes. I just guessed." Termite made reference to the pronghorns fact—the one I had researched the first evening we met—and he giggled.

I put on a smile. Termite always prided himself on his sense of humor, and I wanted to laugh at his last joke for me.

"You were right," I said with a grin.

"I figured I was," Termite said, putting on airs. "You were so young. You would have believed almost anything."

It was true; I had been so young then. I had thought that I had been through life, but I hadn't. Only now had my life brought wisdom.

I looked to Termite. He looked to the distance at his fellow creatures. "Now, you go have fun and always remember how much I love you," I said more to the blackness than him.

"See ya there," Termite said, and headed into the blackness alone.

Tarantula was last in line.

"Hey, Tarantula, how are you feeling?" I asked as I stroked his back. I knew the answer. He was very ill now.

"I'm great," he said, putting on airs for effect. "I'm feeling a lot better. I can't wait for the dance."

"Good, you look a lot better," I lied, and Tarantula shifted positions. He had caught the falsehood.

"Who's the lucky Mrs. Tarantula tonight? I'm sure you could have had any date in the state," I said. I wanted to drag out conversation as long as possible. I did not want to say good-bye.

"There isn't one. I'm going alone," Tarantula said. "I thought I'd hang out with you and Mr. Richard, if you guys don't mind. I talked to Firefly and the three of us are sitting together at the Queen's table."

Tarantula caught my look. "I'm not imposing, am I?" he asked quickly.

I could not lie. Tarantula was one of the most important creatures in my life. I did not want him to remember me that way.

"Mr. Richard is gone."

"What? Where did he go? Is he taking you with him?" Tarantula asked.

"Mr. Richard went very far away, and he wanted desperately to take me with him, Tarantula. He wanted to take me, and he wanted to take you, and all the creatures with him. And he tried really hard. He even had me visit him once to see if I'd like it."

"And did you?" Tarantula asked.

"Oh yes. It was an incredible place that you could only get to through a crystal clear sea. It was a place where everyone was beautiful and healthy. . . ."

"Even me?" Tarantula interrupted.

"Yes, even you would have been healthy there. There were trees out of fairy-tale books, and pools with fire by them so you could never be too hot or too cold. There were tall mountains and stars. The petals of tall flowers provided electricity and people there drank milkshakes, even for breakfast."

"Is Mr. Richard still there?" Tarantula asked.

"He is."

"Is he there by himself?"

"Yes, doll, he's there by himself."

"Why don't you go there?" Tarantula asked.

"Because I can't, Tarantula. That world belongs to Mr. Richard."

Tarantula was silent for a moment.

"Oh," Tarantula said. Understanding.

"Do you want to walk together to the dance then?" Tarantula asked. "I can be your date."

"You know what, I think I'm going to run inside and change into a dress. You go and have fun with your friends. I don't want to cramp your style," I said.

Tarantula began to walk away with his head down. I was worried he would not be able to make it to the Meadows of Lophelia, but had a strong feeling Termite was probably waiting for him a few acres up.

"Mommy?" Tarantula asked when he was almost out of sight.

"Yes," I answered.

"Has anyone ever told you you're beautiful?" he asked. I was glad he was too far to see my tears.

I smiled.

"Yes, Tarantula. And you, you are particularly beautiful," I said.

Tarantula smiled, recognizing Richard's compliment from their first meeting, and hobbled away. When I could no longer see his outline in the distance, I walked toward my glass house.

My only tangible reminder of Richard Dorsey was the stars. I adored them because they reminded me that beauty was always close by. In my life I would never receive gifts as magnificent, but I knew I had to let them go. I picked my stars from the crevices of the greenhouse and carried them outside. Some, the perfect ones chosen by Richard, were keen to shine again. But my stars, the odd-shaped ones with quirky light, squirmed a bit when I suggested they return to their birthplaces. I assured them that they someday would be loved and appreciated and enjoyed.

After I watched the stars return to their places in the sky, I began to pack. It took me less than an hour to collect my simple belongings—clothing, travel kit, a bubblegum lip gloss Zoë had given me, and the occasional knickknack. But my prized possessions had been my creatures and Richard, one of whom I was giving up, and one who had given up on me. The only thing which prevented me from running to the Meadows of Lophelia was my belief that what I was about to do was the best for my creatures. I had been kept in captivity my whole life—slave to a daddy who had forgotten about me, a mama who was sick, a greenhouse full of creatures, a life that was someone else's—and it had almost destroyed me. Richard was a slave, too: to memories, to fear of desertion, to an idyllic era he could not share with the woman he loved lest he lose his ability to run away. Imprisonment had the power to destroy. I did not want anyone, least of all my darling creatures, to be caged anymore.

Hal's Hardware Aluminum Cleaner had a simple label and low price, was easy to apply and foamed nicely. When I was certain the cleaner had been liberally applied, I pulled out a matchbook. The blue-red flame danced on its little black stick, and, despite my many days of preparation, its dance seemed so unplanned. I touched the flame to the aluminum poles and a magical waltz engulfed the life that had engulfed me.

And for just a moment, the sky rained glass.

XXXVIII

The document was in Franklin Gothic and double-spaced. I had spent many hours on the thesis, as I knew it would be the only remainder of Woo Case Study House #1. My report was candid; I said that a glass house could be more constrictive than one of mortar and stone, but I lauded the structure as a singular work of art whose beauty lay in its invisibility.

Kris Tina Woo returned to the Princeton School of Architecture; if rumors were correct, her limited hours outside of the classroom were spent honing her thesis (Dorsey Monument Nine is a chimera!) and drafting detailed blueprints for her next Case Study House, a structure shrouded in secrecy.

The post office was infected with news of the greenhouse fire. Such an event was gossip fodder for a little town like Unity, and I cringed as the townsfolk discussed the fire's origin.

"Hi," I said, careful not to make eye contact. "I have a certified letter which is being held in my name. In addition," I added, "I'm moving and wanted to make sure my mail was held until I have a forwarding address."

The *Unity Ledger* sat on the counter. Kris Tina Woo was pictured on the cover, along with the caption, "Famous architect Kris Tina Woo said that Woo Case Study House #1 had always been her favorite project." Journalistic liberties had obviously been taken.

"Of course," the man said quietly. "I'll be back in a minute."

I glanced surreptitiously at the *Ledger* while my paperwork was processed. Although the front page was obviously dominated by news of the fire, my eye caught a little blurb on the bottom-left corner. I looked closer.

"Famed Designer Dorsey Closes Unity Office."

Richard Dorsey, the world-renowned architect turned interior designer, had been in Unity for seven years, the article said; the sudden move shocked clients and townsfolk alike. Hamilton was quoted ("This town will never be the same. Richard influenced everyone in the know . . .") and the story offered a small black-and-white headshot. Richard was younger when the photo was snapped, perhaps in his midtwenties, and I recognized the photo as a moment from his life with her. He stood beside the Wild Yucca sign and wore his leather motorcycle jacket. His face was tan and windblown, and he was looking at the photographer with a passion that had long ago gone away. I lifted the photograph close to my eyes and stared at it until it was just a series of black and white granular dots that somehow, when they came together, became the most beautiful person in the entire world.

Dorsey's whereabouts were unknown, the article said, and his clients—the list of whom he held in confidence—could not be reached for comment.

The man returned carrying two envelopes. "Is there anything else we can do for you?"

A line had formed behind me.

"Sir," I said in a hush. "How are my creatures? Are they okay?"

"Yes." The old man smiled. "They are fine. Many were interviewed and they vowed to live together in the Meadows of Lophelia. There are trees there for the birds. The Lake of the Exalted Angels is there for the fish, and the rest of the creatures can wander the Meadows. And your tarantula . . ."

My ears perked up.

The postman continued, ". . . that little guy found a girlfriend in no time. There was an empty spot at the Queen's table, and Firefly made certain the prettiest spider in the Meadows sat beside him. She was wearing powder blue, and it was love at first sight."

Tarantula, who had long ago led me to Richard in the '50s aisle, had finally gotten his opportunity to experience what I had that day. I smiled.

Outside, I looked at the envelopes. The first was postmarked in New Jersey. I opened it with a twinge of regret and squinted as I read the words:

Dear Zorka,

Thank you for your relatively insightful thoughts into my tour de force, Woo Case Study House #1. As you are aware, my searches for Architect Dorsey and Dorsey Monument Nine were futile; were it not for the things he left behind— his monuments—I would almost believe my idol had never existed at all.

This letter, I am afraid, also bears catastrophic news. After personally viewing Architect Dorsey's monuments, I have wisely decided to concentrate my efforts on the Craftsman style. Modernism has already been done to perfection; any attempts to emulate (or transcend!) Architect Dorsey's genius will come up short, of this I am certain. Therefore, I will be razing Woo Case Study House #1 in favor of another residence. This process will begin next Tuesday. Thank you in advance for your understanding.

Your Landlord,

Kris Tina Woo

I refolded the letter and smiled. The second envelope stared up at me. My name, first name only, was scribbled hastily; there was no return address. I knew it was not from Richard—he wrote in block letters and in pencil like an architect. I pulled out the sheet of notebook paper.

Below the handwritten line—"I finally arrived at 'Architecture'"—was a scrap torn from *The World Book Encyclopedia*. It read:

Neutra, NOY trah, Richard Joseph (1892–1970) was an Austrian-born architect who settled in the United States in 1925. Neutra's buildings suggest a continuous flow of space by the use of vast sheets of glass and thin supports.

Neutra's best designs demonstrate his goal of creating buildings that meet biological and psychological needs, as well as artistic and technical considerations. In his book *Survival Through Design* (1954), Neutra stated that people could survive only by controlling their environment through design, architecture, and city planning.

y exit from Unity was not poetic in any way. A magnificent sunset did not signify an end to this chapter of my
life. The sky was not cloudy or ominous, to indicate the
move I was about to make was a wrong one. There were no bright
signs with words like "Next Exit to Liberty" or "Construction: Turn
Back!" I wish there were someone in the heavens to point me in the
right direction, to endow me with some celestial road map. But there
was not. I had come this far on my own, and I had learned to expect
that life did not hand out road maps.

Unity held nothing for me now. My mama was buried in Ix with
Daddy's family; even through death her hope burned bright that
Daddy might come back to lie with her for eternity. Daddy, I did not
know where he was. I admit, however, that I still burned a candle for
him, too; there was a plot in that cemetery for me, and I hoped someday to lie between my parents and once again be a family. My creatures were gone to the Meadows of Lophelia. I knew they still
thought of me, and I hoped they were being nice to each other.

As for Richard Dorsey, well, each and every event in my life carried with it a footnote that was Richard Dorsey. Each was followed by

an asterisk, a superscripted number. *See Richard Dorsey. [1]Tell Richard Dorsey. [2]Must do with Richard Dorsey. [3]Richard Dorsey would have appreciated. [4]Cannot stop loving Richard Dorsey. [5]Ibid. [6]Ibid. [7]Ibid. Professors of Latin preached passion for dead romance languages. Pilots expressed love of the air, meteorologists cold fronts, gymnasts balance, research scientists the world. Yet my passion for Richard Dorsey, I am convinced, was felt more deeply than any of these. I often felt as if I were once again in the Wild Yucca swim pool, and Richard was pulling me underwater as he once had pulled her. But the part of this analogy which troubled me the most was that sometimes I felt like I did not want those hands to let go their grasp, lest our hold on each other fall deep into the past, never to return.

Earlier in my life, I would have thought my dorm room at veterinary school to be elegant and fit for a queen. Now, I only found in it style errors. When I arrived, I moved my desk slightly to the left, as Richard would have done, and his exact syntax—"This desk could be kind of brilliant if it faced the north wall"—hung over my mind as a cumulonimbus cloud in a comic strip. I could not sleep and I could not escape him. My nightgown was the one I had last worn in 1959, and the texture, smell, and color reminded me of him. I wondered what the weather was like in 1959, and I wondered what he was doing at this second, and I wondered if there even was a *this second* when two people were so far away from each other. Perhaps he was continuing to design Dorsey Monument Nine, swimming in the swim pool, or imagining life with me. I looked out my window at the moon the shape of a half-eaten pie, and I wondered if, perhaps, Richard Dorsey was looking at the same moon and seeing my reflection in it, as I was seeing his. Perhaps the moon was like a quarter; Richard as its heads and I as its tails.

A glowing ceramic desk lamp waited for me by my side of the bed. I knew it would someday illuminate my future; its light would carry me through long nights of learning the gill structure of the goldfish, the phobias of the domesticated grass snake, the lung capacity of the German shepherd. Yet now the desk lamp only reminded me of the past. A past I did not want yet to turn off.

I knew sleep would not come easily, but I prepared for it anyway. I took the minty toothpaste out of my cloth travel kit and spread it on my toothbrush. I flossed, washed my face, brushed my hair. I did not want to fall alone into my side of a dark bed in a strange place. To procrastinate, I emptied the travel kit, deciding my first night in a lonely dorm was the ideal time to clean out its contents. I had spent close to an hour squeezing my toothpaste until the gel was centered around the cap, winding my floss, and smoothing my lip gloss before I noticed a little piece of paper, folded into a perfectly symmetrical square, resting in the bag's inside pocket. I almost threw it out, assuming it to be a label or cleaning directions, but this was where fate stepped in and did her job. I paused, just before throwing it in the trash, and I slowly unfolded its creases. *Wild Yucca* were the first words I saw. The hotel's name was written in its signature font, the one Richard adored. I read the next line through tears.

In pencil and in sans serif were the words: I love the way you blink your eyes.